Vacation

ON

Union Station

EarthCent Ambassador Series:

Date Night on Union Station

Alien Night on Union Station

High Priest on Union Station

Spy Night on Union Station

Carnival on Union Station

Wanderers on Union Station

Vacation on Union Station

Guest Night on Union Station

Word Night on Union Station

Party Night on Union Station

Review Night on Union Station

Family Night on Union Station

Book Night on Union Station

LARP Night on Union Station

Book Seven of EarthCent Ambassador

Vacation on Union Station

Foner Books

ISBN 978-1-948691-09-3

Copyright 2015 by E. M. Foner

Northampton, Massachusetts

One

"In conclusion, the recent review of EarthCent's policy on earned vacation time, conducted by embassy manager Donna Doogal at the request of our new junior consul, has brought to light the fact that my maternity leave of six years ago was charged against future vacation days, and that the six months I believed I had saved up for a sabbatical existed only in my imagination!"

"You tell them, Ambassador," the aforementioned junior consul egged her on.

Kelly wasn't used to having a human audience for her weekly reports to EarthCent, but somebody had suggested it would be good training for Daniel. Now that she thought about it, that somebody had been Daniel himself. What really set her off about the retroactive policy change was the way it had been discovered. After working just a month, her new assistant had asked Donna to find out if there was a way he could be credited for earned vacation time early, or on credit, as he put it.

"Hopefully, I just did tell them," Kelly replied. "I like to think that less is more when it comes to stating an official grievance, and I doubt it would melt the icy hearts of those human resources fiends to hear how much my children were looking forward to going somewhere."

"That's why I used up all of my vacation time and unpaid educational leave before I began working here," Daniel told her. "I'm an EarthCent brat, you know. My father worked for them until I was nearly ten, so I heard all about the whole pay and benefits thing before I even started."

"I don't think I ever met your father," Kelly said. "Cohan doesn't ring a bell, but if you were ten, that means he retired around twenty-two years ago. I've been with EarthCent for, uh, for a while, and we might have overlapped a couple of years. Just when I was starting out, I mean."

"He didn't retire, he got fired," Daniel told her, though he made it sound like a joke. "My dad was in charge of the bid process to select a terraforming contractor for Venus, and my mom ran a little public relations agency that specialized in representing alien construction consortiums in the Sol system."

"Oh, I may have heard something about that," Kelly said, suddenly feeling embarrassed. "After EarthCent awarded the contract to the Dollnicks, some of the other aliens complained to the president that they had been promised the work in return for cash payments."

"Yeah, that was my parents." Daniel sounded almost proud. "The Stryx didn't care, since my mom was the one who took the money and she didn't work for EarthCent. But old President Lin was worried that spouses selling influence would set a bad precedent, so he and my dad worked out the firing story."

"So he wasn't fired?" Kelly asked.

"Well, he accepted being fired, but he could have refused since he hadn't broken any rules at the time. The truth is, my mom cleared so much money selling imagi-

2

nary influence that they could afford to retire and see the galaxy. My dad still writes long reports about the places they visit, and he sends them back to EarthCent as if he were still working for them. I mentioned it to Clive and Blythe, and after reading the reports from the archives, they told me they have a retirement job for him if he wants it."

"I wondered how you could be so poised with all of the aliens at your age, but that explains it. You spent your youth traveling."

"I met more plants than aliens, though sometimes they're the same thing," Daniel replied. "My parents married while they were still in graduate school, where they were both studying to be evolutionary biologists. My dad still regrets not deferring his start at EarthCent until he finished his degree, but not many people can turn down that invitation. Anyway, he's the one who told me you should always use up your vacation time between postings or they'd come up with a way to take it back."

"Where are your parents now?"

"On some world with breathable air and decent tunnel access. My mom has a theory about meteor-borne microbes that she's trying to piece together by visiting as many planets as possible. I have a hard time imagining that all of the science wasn't sorted out by some species or other a long time ago, but I guess you never know."

"So you went to visit your parents between leaving Middle Station and finally arriving here? I have to admit that I never knew EarthCent would grant unpaid educational leave before the president told me you were taking several months of it. I guess joining your parents in studying alien plants would qualify."

"No, I used my vacation time to visit them. The educational leave was for a study of casino gambling I've been working on since before I joined EarthCent. It's not a degree program or anything, but I was talking about it with Jeeves, and he thinks the Stryx might grant me some sort of certification through their Open University. He also helped me publish my draft findings for alien gambling journalists, and I'm already getting some really good feedback from the Verlocks and the Tharks."

"Is there really anything left to learn about casino games?" Kelly wasn't a fan of gambling, and though she'd finally gotten used to Joe hosting poker games and taking the children to the occasional horse race at the off-world betting parlor, she drew the line at casinos. "I thought the people who owned the casinos had the games all worked out to the last decimal place."

"There aren't many casinos left running house games, like the roulette or blackjack you see in old Earth movies," the junior consul explained. "Well, I take that back. Most casinos still have a version of the slots, basically lottery machines, though every once in a while somebody figures out how to break the latest technology and the manufacturers have to reinvent them from scratch. Between mind control and telekinesis, not to mention out-and-out magic, it's too tough to keep up with cheaters. Most casinos today just provide bonded dealers and a safe environment for gamblers to play each other."

"How does that eliminate cheating?" Kelly inquired.

"It doesn't," Daniel said. "It ensures that the casino makes a steady profit on the table rake and the drinks. Whether or not there's cheating going on is up to the players to figure out. That's where casino security comes in, to keep the gamblers from killing each other."

"Well, I guess if the Stryx recognize your work as educational..." Kelly was dubious about the whole thing, but she wanted to give her new assistant the benefit of the doubt.

"I study how gamblers change their play depending on who else is at the table," Daniel explained. "I lasted almost three months this time with a starting stake of less than a thousand creds. I'd make a good living playing cards if I could figure out a fool-proof way to spot the ringers."

"The professionals pretending to be amateurs?"

"More like the species pretending to be other species," Daniel replied. "I busted out on the last run to an artificial Dollnick who could count into more decks than me. The time before that, it was an old Vergallian woman passing as human. She and my money were two hours gone when the pheromones wore off and I realized she wasn't just making a suggestion when she told me to bet the pot."

"I never really thought about how unscrupulous aliens might be able to take advantage of each other at gambling," Kelly admitted.

"Listen," Daniel said, satisfied that he had successfully defended his hobby and returning to the prior subject. "If the home office won't reverse their decision about maternity leave, you should just go on vacation and not tell them. Anything I can't handle, I can always take to InstaSitter."

"You mean EarthCent Intelligence," Kelly corrected him.

"They should change the display in the corridor if they want me to call it that." The junior consul shot her one of his patented boyish grins. "Besides, every time I go there, I get mobbed by three-year-olds."

"My two godchildren do not constitute a mob," Libby interjected over the office speakers. "Nor can their actions in welcoming you in any way be construed as mobbing."

"That's my cue." The junior consul got up, brushed the wrinkles out of his suit pants, and headed for the door. "See you all on Monday."

"Bye," Kelly called after him. Daniel Cohan was such a complete change from Aisha that she sometimes forgot that he worked for her and not the other way around. A young-looking thirty-two, he never seemed to lack confidence in what he was doing, and unlike Kelly, he had no problem with forgetting about work the moment he walked out the embassy door. Maybe that would change some day if he became an ambassador, but she wouldn't bet on it, and not just because she disapproved of gambling.

"I'm sorry to hear you've been impacted by the retroactive changes to EarthCent's vacation policy," the station librarian told Kelly once they were alone. "We've been trying to shift some of the EarthCent personnel decisions to humans, and part of that process involves not looking over their shoulders."

"Well, I wish you'd go back to the old system, then," Kelly said. "I'd head for Earth myself and give whoever created that policy a piece of my mind, but it appears I can't afford the time off."

"What about Daniel's suggestion? Take a vacation and don't tell anybody."

"I don't want to set a bad example for my children, or Daniel for that matter. Besides, as much as I hate to admit it, we were having a hard time coming up with somewhere we really wanted to go. I guess Joe and I have become Union Station homebodies."

"There are worse things," Libby said, and the ambassador clearly heard a smile in the Stryx's synthesized voice. "I haven't gone anywhere in hundreds of thousands of years myself. Why don't you take a month off from work without leaving the station? Under the current EarthCent rules for ambassadors, it doesn't count as a vacation as long as you remain onboard your posting."

"Are you serious, Libby? I could stop coming into the embassy every day and they'd have to keep paying me?"

"Ambassadors are officially on call twenty-four hours a day as long as they're on the station. That's how the job is defined. I wouldn't necessarily recommend telling EarthCent that you aren't coming in to the office, but Daniel and Donna can handle any visitors to the embassy. If anything comes up that really does require your presence, you're no further away by lift tube than you would be if you were at home."

"Where would I be if not at home?" Kelly asked. "I mean, we both know that EarthCent owes me that vacation time and I'd just be taking back what's really mine, but I can't leave the station, and it would be silly to go stay in a hotel. I doubt we could even find one that would accept Beowulf."

"Jeeves tells me that Dorothy and Samuel are both a good age for camping and exploring, and I'm sure Gryph would give you access to some of the uninhabited areas of the station. You know that he keeps plenty of decks in reserve against biological emergencies, and when a sentient race abandons a section for whatever the reason, he doesn't hurry to recycle it for another species. You never know if their descendants might make a comeback and return to the tunnel network, not to mention that it would be a crime to simply dispose of viable flora and fauna."

"Are you telling me that I've lived on this station for nearly seventeen years and I never knew that it was half empty?" Kelly demanded.

"I seem to recall that you lived on the station for at least a dozen years before you found out that the deck above this one is occupied by the Cherts," Libby reminded her. "Of course, it's not like you could have stumbled across any of the areas I'm talking about on your own, since the lift tubes wouldn't take you there without Gryph's permission."

"But would the children really enjoy it? If this deck was unoccupied, I wouldn't want to come here on vacation. What would we do? Wander around the empty shops and corridors? I suppose an unoccupied ag deck might be nice for hiking, but it would be awfully quiet."

"Talk it over with Joe and the kids," Libby suggested. "Most of the children on the station tell each other scary stories about the hidden decks, the same way you might have talked about haunted houses when you were young."

"You wouldn't have a, uh, brochure I could show my family for any of these places, would you?" Kelly thought she managed to keep the suspicion out of her voice and substituted "brochure" for "something in writing" at the last second, but Libby noticed her hesitation.

"You don't trust me to pick out a nice vacation spot for you."

Nothing made Kelly feel as guilty as when Libby intentionally flattened out her artificially generated voice to remove the emotional content. It was as if the Stryx librarian was throwing up barriers to hide being hurt.

"Of course I trust you, Libby. It's just that picking out a place to go is one of the best parts of a vacation. I remember my parents telling me that when they were children, there used to be regional tourism offices you could write away to, and then you would get brochures in the mail from dozens of campsites and local attractions. That was more than seventy years ago, but it sounded really fun."

"Would you settle for a holo presentation?"

"Of course," Kelly replied, realizing she'd trapped herself. It wasn't that she thought the station librarian would misrepresent the possible destinations, but Libby had a way of staging her presentations so that there didn't seem to be any doubt as to which option was the correct choice.

"I'll have something ready for you by the time you get home from Chastity's house-warming party," Libby said, instantly back to her usual, cheerful self.

"Drat! I knew I was late for something!" Kelly cried, jumping up from her desk. "And Donna reminded me to get ready right before she went home. They're very happy with the influence Marcus is having on Chastity. She left Tinka in charge of InstaSitter during the honeymoon, and she hasn't rushed back into working seven days a week."

"I think you'll be impressed with their home," Libby commented. "It's the only human residence on the station with a full dance floor. Chastity got permission from Gryph to cut in a separate entrance so Marcus can give private lessons."

"I don't think I'd want my new husband teaching a bunch of single women how to dance," Kelly said. "She must really trust him."

"The studio features the latest in immersive recording technology so that the students can practice the same steps at home with a hologram. Of course, Chastity will have a live feed to her office, just in case she misses her husband while she's at work and wants to check in."

"Doveryai, no proveryai," Kelly quoted over her shoulder on her way out of the office. "Trust, but verify."

"She did go to my school, after all," Libby said proudly.

Two

"I'm fine with taking care of Mac's Bones while you're gone, as long as somebody else handles all of the training camp stuff," Paul assured his foster father. "Maybe we'll join you for a whole weekend here and there if Aisha can get the time off from the Grenouthians, but she's in the middle of the season. How long do you have before Kelly needs to be back for her next show?"

"She decided against doing any more live broadcasts and they already prerecorded the next episode," Joe replied. "She was in the studio with the Verlock ambassador working on it all day yesterday. I don't know why it never occurred to me, but it turns out that Ambassador Srythlan can only keep up with alien conversations thanks to special training. Even with the best implants, most Verlocks can't easily participate in back-and-forth discussions with other species because we all talk too fast."

"I thought they only spoke slowly, but I guess it makes sense that they'd be accustomed to hearing language at the same speed they grew up speaking it. So how do the Grenouthians work around it?"

"The Verlocks don't move much faster than they speak, so for some shows, the Grenouthians can just slow the whole thing down and nobody complains. But for immersives where the motion has to take place at full

11

speed, the Verlocks prefer captions to audio translations. Apparently they're very fast readers."

"Which approach did 'Ask An Alien' go with?"

"Kelly said that a large part of the audience for this interview is likely to be Verlocks, so the Grenouthians decided to do two versions. Srythlan answered the questions at his native speed, and for the non-Verlock broadcast, they'll just speed him up. For the Verlock edition, they'll slow Kelly down. Since it's not live, it doesn't matter that the Verlock version will be three times as long."

"The bunnies are probably thrilled with the extra commercial time," Paul said.

"You've forgotten the second law of thermodynamics," Joe pointed out. "The Verlock commercials run three times as slow."

"You're applying the conservation of energy to advertising?" Before he even finished asking, Paul realized that his foster father was just teasing and decided to get him back. "Anyway, how are you going to get beer while you're off on station safari?"

"You're going to send it to me," Joe replied seriously. "Libby asked Gryph to assign us a maintenance bot for the duration, sort of a private delivery service. It's not like we could have carried along a month's worth of food or foraged off of alien agriculture."

"You're calling it a camping trip but you're planning to live on take-out?"

"I already made a deal with Ian to send us their catering leftovers at a discount, so it should be an adventure in eating as well."

"Which deck are you going to start with?" Paul asked, now that it was clear that the family would be vacationing in style. "I saw the choices when Kelly replayed them for

Aisha, and some of those abandoned alien sections looked pretty interesting. I asked Jeeves about them, but he said he didn't want to spoil any surprises."

"Kelly and the kids couldn't agree, so they decided to let Libby pick for them."

"You didn't get a vote?"

"I've already been to more places than I care to remember," Joe replied. "I'm just happy to be able to take Dorothy and Samuel on vacation without having to get them a bunch of inoculations against flesh-eating bacteria. And thank you for talking your wife into letting us bring Ailia along."

"It wasn't a hard sell in the end. It wouldn't have been any fun for the girl to hang around Mac's Bones after school with just me and Dring for company. Aisha doesn't think it's appropriate to take Ailia to work when she's not in the cast rotation."

"Now that's all settled, are you going to be around for the game?" Joe asked. "Herl is coming tonight, and he always has a couple interesting tricks up his tentacle."

"Aisha and I are taking the kids out to dinner and an immersive," Paul said. "It's supposedly the first Earth production to gain any traction with the alien audiences, something about children and dragons bonding together as warrior pairs to fight an invasion."

"I hope it's not too scary for Samuel and Ailia," Joe said. "Samuel only turned six a couple weeks ago."

"Aisha got all of the details from the Grenouthian distributor. It's based on the first part of some old series that's seven books long, and the invasion doesn't happen until the last book. They're only making one every other year so they can show the actors growing up. Samuel will be done with school by the time it gets bloody."

13

"I sort of remember seeing a movie series when I was a kid that had been made that way," Joe said. "My parents told me that there was a time when the release of a new sequel was a big event, with people lining up outside of theatres in the middle of the night to be the first to get tickets."

Paul put a hand to his ear, a courtesy gesture many humans used when carrying on a subvoced discussion over implants. He seemed to be listening more than replying, and finally he said out loud, "I'll be right there."

"Something wrong?" Joe asked.

"Just my brain," Paul replied. "Aisha and the kids are waiting for me in the Little Apple. I thought we were meeting here. See you later."

Paul jogged off towards the exit from Mac's Bones, and Joe busied himself setting up for the poker game. He put out the chips and found a fresh deck of cards. Then he remembered that Kelly had volunteered to help Donna set up for the monthly EarthCent mixer and would no doubt fill up on free finger food from the caterers. He went into the kitchen and made a meal out of leftovers for himself, though most of it ended up in Beowulf's stomach. Then the man and the reincarnated dog took a stroll around Mac's Bones to see if there were any last-minute emergencies before the card players began arriving. Three hours later, Joe was beginning to wish that one of the campers had flagged him down for an urgent repair.

"Are you two playing teams or something?" Lynx asked Shaina, throwing down her cards in disgust. "Every time Jeeves drops out of the bidding, you take the pot, and every time you drop out, he takes it."

"We just know each other's style from playing countless hands on the auction circuit," Shaina explained. She raked the pot into her large pile, leaving a ten millicred chip in the middle of the table to ante for the next hand. "You're lucky Brinda isn't here tonight because she and Jeeves are practically telepathic."

"You're just making excuses because you can't accept that your sister has a better poker face than you do," Jeeves told his business partner. "It's a wonder she doesn't bluff every hand, given your inability to read her."

"Can I deal this time, or am I still on gofer duty?" Daniel asked. It seemed that whenever the cards came his way, Joe sent him to refill the pitcher, explaining that the house went by mercenary rules, where the youngest did all of the running. When the junior consul returned from his last trip to the brew room, he found Beowulf sitting next to his chair, glumly shaking his massive head. Fortunately, the Huravian hound had folded Daniel's hand rather than trying to draw to an inside straight, so the beer run only cost him his ante.

"I guess we can let you give it a try," Joe replied. "My luck can't get any worse. Just don't call any of that one-eyed jacks and suicide kings nonsense."

"Actually, I was kind of hoping to talk you guys into a hand of Rainbow," Daniel insinuated. "Any objections?"

"I don't have a Horten deck," Joe said.

"I brought my own." The junior consul pulled a fat box out of an inner pocket and shook out the alien deck. He smiled self-consciously before springing all of the cards from one hand to the other in a magician's arc.

In his best imitation of a Wild West saloon gambler, Woojin drawled, "I think we got us a card sharp, Joe. Last time I saw anybody do that at a poker game, it ended in a knife fight."

"Not in my house," Kelly called from the couch, without looking up from her book. Joe and Woojin exchanged glances. Neither of them missed the bad old days, but there were times when the poker games in Mac's Bones with the ambassador in the wings seemed just a little too tame.

"Does everybody know the rules?" Daniel inquired, pausing before he dealt.

"What kind of Drazen would know the rules to a Horten card game?" Herl asked, doing his best to look offended.

"The spymaster kind," Lynx retorted. "I've seen you in the casino."

"Rainbow it is," Daniel announced, and began dealing the cards around to the eight players. "In deference to my elders, I won't call any wilds, but these are genuine Horten cards, not the cheap Dollnick knock-offs."

"You mean they can change color spontaneously?" Shaina asked. "I've heard of them, of course, but I've never played with the genuine article."

"It's not exactly spontaneous, they're just trying to blend in," Woojin explained. "If you have four red ones, a blue one and a white one, they might all eventually turn pink. So if you keep the bidding going long enough, a garbage hand could turn into a flush, or a straight into a straight flush."

"Don't help her," Lynx said gruffly. "She's already got half of our chips."

"Now who's playing teams," Shaina replied archly. "Thank you, Woojin. I'll keep that in mind when your fiancée is bidding."

"Hang on," Herl said. "Somebody didn't ante."

"Dealer doesn't ante in Horten games," Daniel informed him. "Are you sure you've played this before?"

"Of course, of course," the Drazen spymaster said, but he looked and sounded rather like a confused old man. Five minutes later, he looked like a happy, middle-aged gambler raking in a pot.

"I can't believe I fell for that," Lynx groaned. She began stacking her remaining chips by color to see how far she was down. "Of course, of course," she mimicked the Drazen. "I'm just a poor old spymaster in over his head who doesn't even know the rules to the game."

"My cards never changed color," Jeeves complained. "If the white one had just turned blue, I would have had a higher straight flush than Herl."

"Maybe you didn't want it hard enough," Shaina suggested.

"I don't think it's fair that I have to abstain from using my natural talents while the rest of you are allowed to affect the color of the cards with your emotions. I vote that artificial intelligences at these games be allowed to employ one non-memory-related advantage."

The humans and the Drazen all extended a hand with a thumb pointed down.

"It's not like you ever go home a loser," Lynx said. "If we let you start reading skin temperatures or applying facial analysis algorithms, you'd have a catalog of tells as good as reading our minds. Besides, you could just skip any future Horten hands or let Beowulf sit in for you."

"Nix on that," Joe interrupted. "If I have to choose between Jeeves reading my skin temperature and Beowulf sniffing out my emotions, I'll go with Jeeves every time. Besides, you don't want to be in the same room if that hound loses a big pot. He never could stop himself from going all-in on aces."

"It's my deal," Woojin said, retrieving the standard deck of cards and shuffling. "Five card stud, everyone antes, no blinds."

"Did I mention that some guy tried to get me to sign an anti-EarthCent petition in the Little Apple at lunch today?" Daniel asked. The game stalled while Woojin picked up the cards after misfiring on an attempt to imitate the junior consul's card trick. "He seemed to think we're collaborating with the Stryx to repress him."

"Here, on the station?" Kelly looked up from her book again. "Why didn't you tell me?"

"You and Donna were out all afternoon setting up for the dance thing," Daniel reminded her. "I invited the guy to come to the embassy next week and talk to us about it, but who knows if he'll show up."

"Did he sound sane?" Kelly asked. "We've had complaints about EarthCent from time to time, but never a petition."

"He was very polite, and his suit looked expensive," Daniel said. "Do you get a lot of political protests here?"

"This is the first one I've heard about," Kelly replied. "I don't get it at all. If he doesn't trust us or the Stryx, what's he planning to do with all of the signatures? I remember reading about petitions somewhere, and the whole point was to deliver them to whoever is in authority."

"I guess I should have taken the time to read it, but I was too hungry," Daniel said. "He mentioned that he only arrived yesterday, so it's hard to imagine that he has anything against the Union Station embassy in particular. He did say some pretty harsh things about the tyranny of the unelected, though."

"Did you hear that, Joe?" Kelly asked. "Somebody told Daniel that I'm a tyrant."

"I'm sitting right here, Kel, you don't have to say everything twice," Joe responded in exasperation. "Are you sure you don't want to try a hand?"

"No. You know how I feel about gambling," Kelly replied, looking down at her book again. It seemed like she'd been on the same page for a half an hour.

"This may be a red herring, but I watch the mercenary job boards just to keep up with the flow, and I've seen a number of human settlements posting requests for police contractors in the last few days," Woojin said. He paused to deal out the first two cards. "I was going to bring it up with Clive when I had enough data points, but the interesting thing is who was placing the ads."

"You just told us," Lynx said. "Human settlements."

"The work was on human settlements, but in all of the ads the contact person was listed as a mayor or executive of some sort. I've never been to a human settlement with an executive form of government. Even those two off-network colony worlds we visited, Kibbutz and Bits, handled everything informally."

"It makes sense that independent groups of humans who find they require a government would look to their history for precedents," Herl said. He peeked at his hole-card and grimaced. "I believe that Drazen cities had something like mayors before we began settling other worlds."

"How does colonizing space change the need for government?" Lynx asked. "If anything, I would have guessed that frontier worlds and colonies would have even more need of a strong executive. I used to go armed and worry about losing my cargo to criminals when trading took me to those places."

"By the time we developed faster-than-light capability and joined the tunnel network, we'd had a much longer time to mature than humans," Herl replied modestly. "At some point, your typical species discovers that the most economically efficient way to run a community is to get along with one another. The infrastructure and service providers who collect fees are the closest thing to local government on most Drazen worlds. While we aren't immune to crime, it's handled by our planetary defense forces."

"My cards tonight are a crime," Joe growled, refilling his glass from the pitcher.

"So you're saying that thanks to the Stryx, humans have gone from hitting each other over the head with rocks to flying around the stars, without having the time to become civilized?" Lynx asked.

"The effort required to develop the science and technology for even the crudest jump-drives requires a high degree of cooperation," Herl replied. "Was there ever a time that humans were willing to invest half of their economic output into something that would take generations to accomplish?"

"Aren't there any aliens who figure out the science stuff for themselves before they're ready for it?" Kelly asked.

"Would you at least please come and sit with us if you're going to participate in the conversation?" Joe begged his wife. "I'm getting a sore neck looking over at you every two minutes."

"I'm reading," Kelly replied, but she waited for Herl's answer.

"Technology outpacing maturity is one of the defining factors for unstable species," Herl replied. "It doesn't always end badly, of course, but many of those species who survive long enough to join the tunnel network end up retiring back to their own worlds because they can't get along with the rest of us."

"The rest of you can get along without me for a hand," Joe said in disgust, mucking his cards and rising from the table. "Kelly, I'm getting you a chair."

"I don't want to interfere with your game," Kelly protested, but she came over to the table and took Joe's vacated seat. "Have you heard about any problems with humans committing crimes in Drazen space, Herl?"

"Raise ten," the Drazen spymaster said, tossing a yellow chip into the pot. Everybody except for Jeeves and Woojin folded. "To be perfectly honest with you, I doubt we'd notice. The only places in Drazen space with high concentrations of humans are consortium-managed worlds, and they handle their own policing internally, as a business expense."

Woojin gave each of the two remaining players another face-up card and then dealt one to himself. He and Jeeves both looked to the Drazen for the bet.

"Pass," Herl muttered.

Jeeves tapped the table with his pincer.

"I'll raise twenty," Woojin said, throwing two yellow chips in the pot. Lynx tried to peek at his hole card, but he slapped her hand away. "No free samples until after the wedding," he told her. Herl folded his hand, but Jeeves pushed two yellows into the pot to call.

Woojin dealt a third open card to Jeeves, who paired his exposed seven. The dealer paired his five. The Stryx and the ex-mercenary regarded each other across the table for a long minute, and then Jeeves tapped with his pincer. Woojin slid him the final card without raising, and then dealt one to himself. Neither player improved their hand by the cards that were showing.

"Pass," Jeeves said.

Woojin hesitated, toying with his stacks and picking up a blue chip, which was worth a whole cred. Then he dropped it and flipped over his face cards, conceding the pot.

"You beat me with what you've got showing," he remarked.

"That makes no sense," Kelly complained. "Why did Herl raise and then drop out, and then you raised and dropped out, and neither of you could beat a pair of sevens? With eight players, I'd think somebody would always get a better hand than that."

"Hoping for the best can get expensive," Lynx told her. Then she turned to Herl and asked, "Did you know about all of the empty decks on the station?"

"We don't really pay that much attention to Stryx affairs," the Drazen spymaster replied. "I do know that all of the stations I've visited are continually undergoing new construction, but it plays out so slowly in biological time that migrations are rare."

"Migrations?" Kelly asked.

"When they slow the spin rate," Herl explained. "The Stryx never build into the hollow core of the station, they add decks to the outer hull. The core radius is large enough that each new deck isn't moving that much faster than the one below it, but every few million years, there are enough new decks that they have to let the rotational rate decay a bit. Otherwise, the angular acceleration at the outer hull would keep creeping up, and it would be hard

22

to find biological tenants who were comfortable carrying that much weight around."

"Why keep building with all of the empty decks?" Shaina asked.

"Keeps the bots in practice," Jeeves said, performing a one-handed deck manipulation with his pincer. "Are we still playing?"

"I seem to remember hearing of an early Grenouthian documentary series about the unoccupied decks on one of the stations," Herl commented, moving his ante into the center of the table.

"Libby?" Kelly inquired out loud. "Do you remember a documentary about the empty decks on stations?"

"Hidden Treasures of the Stryx," the librarian replied scornfully. "It was more of an exercise in showmanship than a documentary. The Grenouthians promoted each new episode for cycles in advance. They featured interviews with questionable historians, and speculative reenactments of lurid episodes attributed to whatever species once occupied the deck. By the time they got around to actually sending in an immersive crew and finding an empty field or pile of abandoned junk, the viewers didn't care anymore because the Grenouthians had already started teasing the next episode."

"Did they feature any of the decks we'll be visiting?" Kelly asked.

"That show was shot on Corner Station. I have no idea why Farth ever gave the Grenouthians access in the first place, but it was over a hundred thousand years ago, and none of the first generation Stryx have seen the need to repeat the experiment." Libby replied.

Joe returned to the table with a chair dangling from one hand and bowl of pretzels in the other. Beowulf waited for

23

the owner of Mac's Bones to sit, at which point the dog came over and dropped his head on the man's lap, waiting for a salt fix. "Are you playing my chips or should I raid the bank for you?" Joe asked his wife.

"I'm just reading," Kelly asserted, looking around for her book. When she realized she'd left it behind on the couch, she gave in and reached for Joe's pile. "It's not my money so it's not really gambling," she justified herself. "But, Libby? Warn me when the kids get out of the lift tube."

Three

"Thank you all for attending on such short notice," Kelly said, glancing at the top right of the hologram to make sure that encryption was turned on. "Director Oxford will be joining us in a few minutes, but I thought it would make sense to take a vote first on whether or not this falls within the scope of activity for an intelligence agency."

"I realize I'm the new kid on the block, but I'm a little puzzled by the timing of this meeting," said Ambassador Fu. "I think the self-government issue is certainly worth discussing, but I wish we had been given a little more notice to prepare."

Kelly turned to her left to address the Void Station ambassador, even though the holo-conference technology always processed the holograms so that everybody thought that everybody else was looking at them. The effect was rather like sitting around a conference table peopled with Old Masters portraits, since the eyes seem to follow the observer around the room.

"It came to my own attention just recently, and it occurred to me that asking our intelligence people to look into accusations that we're running some sort of police state could create a conflict of interest," Kelly replied.

"Well, you all know that I'm in no hurry to see EarthCent getting into the military business," Ambassador

25

White said. "But that does appear to be how most of the advanced species handle their policing, so perhaps we should look into it." Belinda White was dressed in what looked like an old British safari outfit, and Kelly wondered if she was heading to a costume party right after the conference.

"I learned of an active anti-EarthCent movement on Middle Station earlier today," Carlos Oshi contributed. "My weekly meeting with the local council of merchants was interrupted by a group of human demonstrators, though they weren't as well prepared as one might expect. I'd like to play a recording of that event made by our station librarian."

"It's your committee, Kelly," President Beyer said.

"You have the hologram," Kelly told Ambassador Oshi.

A scene from Middle Station showing a large café in a setting modeled after an Italian piazza popped into life over Kelly's display desk. Ambassador Oshi was standing at a makeshift lectern looking bemused as a group of protesters armed with placards pushed into the space between the tables where the local business leaders were sitting. One protester held an old-fashioned megaphone and led the chants.

"We want free elections," the woman shouted.

"We want free elections," the protesters repeated dutifully.

"No representation without participation," proclaimed the leader.

"No representation without participation," the followers echoed.

"Stryx go home!" she shouted.

"Stryx go home?"

26

The protesters repeated this last bit uncertainly, and a young man let his sign fall and raised a hand.

"Yes, Jason?" the leader said through her megaphone. She was plainly unhappy with the interruption, but as an advocate of participatory government, she had encouraged her followers to ask questions at any time.

"Aren't the Stryx already home?" Jason asked. "I mean, they own the stations and all."

"That's an excellent observation, young man," Ambassador Oshi interjected before the protest leader could reply. "I'd be happy to address all of your questions if you'll meet with me at the embassy later. Right now we're in the middle of a meeting to raise funds for a children's theatre."

"Oh, sorry," the young man said. The other protesters let their signs droop and some of them looked rather abashed. "My little brother wants to be an actor. Can I do anything to help?"

"Jason!" the leader shouted through her megaphone. "Don't let the oppressors buy you off with their bread and circuses. Have you forgotten what I said in our meeting just twenty minutes ago?"

"But now we're interrupting their meeting, Amber," protested a middle-age woman. The sign which she had allowed to slide to the floor read, "One sentient, one vote."

"Did anybody ask us for our input on this alleged theatre project?" Amber shouted back through her megaphone. "Who are they to decide for all of the humans living on the station?"

"Do you have something against children's theatre?" Jason asked.

"It's not about the damned children's theatre!" Amber yelled, losing her temper. "It's about self-determination and not living as slaves of the Stryx overlords."

"Are you feeling alright, Miss, er, Amber?" Ambassador Oshi inquired. He appeared to be genuinely concerned. "Waiter? Could you bring the young lady a glass of water?"

Amber snarled at him, raised her megaphone to say something, and then changed her mind and marched off, head held high. The rest of the protesters melted away. The scene vanished and the hologram of the steering committee members seated around a virtual conference table returned.

"Wow," Belinda said. "That was really wild."

"I suspect those protesters had less time to prepare for their demonstration than I did for this meeting," the Void Station ambassador observed.

"Has anybody else experienced a similar outbreak of democracy?" the president asked with a crooked smile.

"I did have an awkward meeting earlier this week with a local man who wanted to register his candidacy for the next ambassadorial election," Ambassador Zerakova said. "I tried to explain to him that we don't have elections, but it didn't seem to sink in. He kept posing the same question in different ways until finally I sent him to dinner with my junior consul. It couldn't have gone very well because she hasn't been speaking to me for the last two days."

"Does the close timing of these incidents strike anybody else as suspicious?" Belinda asked. "Why don't we get our Mr. Oxford's opinion on all of this before we make any decisions? That is what we pay him for, after all."

"He's waiting in my outer office, so we'll skip the vote and invite him in now if there are no objections," Kelly said. "Oh, and just in case you've forgotten, we don't pay him. The intelligence agency supports itself by selling data and services to the business community."

"Could a police force be self-funding?" the president asked.

"For much of Earth's history they practically were, at least in some countries," Svetlana replied. "Of course, it meant that police protection was primarily available to those who could afford it, and the biggest spenders were organized crime bosses."

Clive entered Kelly's office during this last exchange and took the seat across from her at the display desk. The holo-controller made a space for him at the virtual conference table between Belinda and Svetlana, rearranging them all in a boy-girl pattern for some obscure reason of its own.

"I believe I know all of you except for the gentleman in the nightgown," Clive said, looking around the hologram.

"They're pajamas," Ambassador Fu replied. "I am Zhao Fu, and I was appointed the Void Station ambassador after Mr. Beyer accepted the EarthCent presidency."

"Clive Oxford, pleased to make your acquaintance," the director of EarthCent Intelligence introduced himself briskly. "I overheard the last couple comments about funding for a police force as I came in, and I can confirm that self-funding would lead to distortions in enforcement policy. I know that in the case of mercenaries, granting charters to attack enemy shipping usually turns into out-and-out piracy. But first I'd like to present our current assessment of the human-on-human crime situation and discuss whether there's really a need for policing in some human communities."

"Please do," President Beyer said.

"EarthCent has escaped the problem of policing humanity in space to this point thanks to the fact that practically all of the humans who have left Earth are living as guests or contract workers. This means that they, we, live under alien authorities whose surveillance and enforcement technologies make it nearly impossible for human criminals to avoid detection and capture."

"I can see where that would discourage property crime, and of course, none of the Earth's laws regarding vice have any meaning to aliens, but what about violent crime?" Belinda asked.

"Human-on-human crimes against persons are indeed the main problem under alien rule," Clive replied. "But you have to remember that the humans living on alien worlds have no rights other than those granted by the landlords. I'm sure you all see your share of runaways from labor contracts, especially the young people who grew up in the system rather than making a commitment of their own accord. I'm also sure you all have friends or acquaintances who were contract laborers at one time or another, but have you ever heard somebody complain about the alien policing?"

"An interesting point," the Middle Station ambassador commented. "We conduct an ongoing survey of humans transiting the station, mainly questions about their employment experiences, though you can find most of the same information on the job boards run by the laborer agencies. The food, the pay, the hours, and the conduct of their co-workers all come in for regular criticism. Occasionally we're asked to look into a failure to deliver on promised bonuses, but I can't recall the issue of policing coming up even once."

"Even if it was an issue, we have no jurisdiction in alien space to do anything about it," Clive pointed out. "The Stryx grant us limited self-government on our own decks, but since they also provide all of the infrastructure and services, there's never been a need for anything beyond the business associations and school cooperatives. The only place we see a real demand for policing is on the self-governing human colonies and outposts. As more humans who complete labor contracts opt to remain in space rather than retiring to Earth, the human populations on the open worlds of the tunnel network are starting to grow rapidly."

"But the open worlds still belong to the aliens, don't they?" Ambassador Fu inquired. "I'm not aware of any sovereign human worlds on the tunnel network."

"Ahem," President Beyer cleared his throat meaningfully.

"Aside from Earth, of course," the new ambassador amended himself hastily.

"Open worlds weren't an option for humans until just a few years ago," Clive explained. "It takes money to buy passage and land, not to mention capital to invest in setting up a farm or a business. Generally speaking, unless the world is well established, newcomers are expected to handle their own affairs. The open worlds currently accepting humans are owned by Dollnick merchant princes, Drazen consortiums and of course, the Verlocks. But it's rare for any other species to want to live anywhere a Verlock would feel comfortable."

"I've heard the Dollnicks hire human laborers for terraforming projects, and when the world is ready for occupation, they try to recover their investment by selling part of the real estate to the same laborers who did the work," President Beyer said.

"It seems to be a successful business model," Clive replied. "From the human standpoint, it saves on transportation costs if they remain on the world where they or their parents served out a labor contract, and they also know exactly what to expect."

"But I suppose when they move from a work camp or a company town into an independent human settlement, the Dollnicks are no longer responsible for policing," Belinda said. "Do you have any information on how they're coping?"

"Everything we know to date comes from an analysis of the help-wanted ads posted to the mercenary exchanges," Clive said. "We've assigned a pair of senior agents to visit some representative communities and to talk things over with whoever is in charge. The ads usually state that the humans are willing to consider proposals from artificial people and aliens, but for the money they're offering, the only takers will be human, or perhaps some Gem ex-military. By contrast, doing police work on alien outposts has always been viewed as desirable work for human mercenaries, but of course, the aliens can afford to pay well."

"Why would any of the advanced species need human cops?" the president asked.

"It mainly comes down to economics," Clive explained. "None of the advanced species hire mercenaries for policing on developed worlds, or even on their own colonies, for that matter. Most of the demand is from mining outposts, recreational orbitals and commercial ag worlds. The only aliens who go to live at those places are doing it as a job, or on mining outposts, for a chance to strike it rich on shares. If they want to work as police, they prefer to do it somewhere civilized."

"I recall that you started out as a mercenary, Director Oxford," Svetlana said. "Did you have any experiences in this field?"

"I worked as a market cop on a Frunge orbital for six months," Clive replied. "It was even more depressing than fighting in the endless Vergallian wars. As on the Stryx stations, Frunge surveillance made it nearly impossible to get away with committing a crime undetected, so there's little point in trying unless the criminal has the means to immediately flee into space. My platoon was responsible for investigating transient-on-transient crimes, but the Frunge had a different system to address problems with their own citizens."

"Do you believe we should be encouraging the humans on these open worlds to set up their own surveillance societies?" Raj inquired.

"That's above my pay grade," Clive responded. "I can only tell you that the near-certainty of being detected tends to remove the profit motive from most crimes. The advanced species have their problems, but other than the feuds and the occasional crime of passion, it's mostly sophisticated stuff, more like industrial espionage than smash-and-grab. The kind of police work that human mercenaries are capable of doing for aliens is of the frontier town variety, or anti-piracy patrols."

"We recently had an unfortunate incident involving some of the youth on our lower deck overdosing on stimulants for recreational purposes," said Svetlana. "Pepper is manufactured by the Farlings and tailored for human biology. It provides a feeling of energy and wakefulness with no noticeable side effects right up to the third or fourth day when the user collapses."

"Collapsing sounds like a pretty serious side effect to me," Kelly said.

"Users can avoid that part if they take what amounts to an antidote at the right time," Svetlana explained. "Of course, the antidote, Salt, is priced higher than the Pepper, and it also puts you to sleep for twenty-four hours or so."

"Is there a big difference between collapsing in bed and taking the antidote?" President Beyer asked.

"The users who take Salt according to the schedule seem to hold up pretty well, but the ones who only use Pepper lose weight, and their hair starts falling out almost immediately," the Corner Station ambassador replied. "It's the hair loss that's kept this drug from turning into an epidemic. According to our station librarian, the drugs aren't sufficiently harmful to fall under a Stryx import ban, and are probably safe if used as directed."

"I think we should talk to the Dollnicks about this," Kelly said. "They may not be the largest employer of human labor in terms of the total numbers, but their projects are certainly the biggest. I'm aware of an ongoing terraforming job where the Dollys have more than thirty million humans at work on a single planet, and that doesn't include the dependents."

"I'll ask our local Dollnick ambassador," Raj Tamil offered. "They employ tens of millions of humans on a pair of ag worlds they run in a nearby system, and I was able to help the ambassador with recruiting the latest replacements. It seems that the market for unskilled human laborers has become more competitive since most of the people who wanted off of Earth have left."

"Speaking of Dollnick terraforming and human emigration, how long until Venus is available?" Belinda asked.

"That project is strictly in the chemical lab phase," the president replied. "The Dollnicks are still working at removing the sulfuric acid from the atmosphere, after which I believe the plan is to mechanically sequester most of the carbon dioxide before they introduce specially engineered microbes to start the real terraforming process. We'll all be long dead before any humans set foot on the surface."

"Again, I apologize in advance if I'm bringing up a point which has previously been discussed by this committee, but policing and intelligence gathering are very different activities," Ambassador Fu stated. "My understanding is that our intelligence service grew out of EarthCent's need for information to help our diplomats, including those present. A commitment to policing, however, requires both enforcement and a judiciary to deal with suspected criminals, not to mention a penal system."

"We don't have any budget for a judiciary or prisons," President Beyer cautioned the group. "We don't even have the authority to raise money beyond the funding we get from the Stryx."

"Couldn't we just dump the bad apples on a Wanderer fleet?" the Middle Station ambassador asked.

"It doesn't work that way," Kelly said. "The mobs only come around every few hundred years, and they don't accept just anybody."

"Maybe we could extend the successful model of the Stryx stations, where all of the policing is done by bots," Svetlana suggested. "I realize that they are being controlled by the station manager, but perhaps we could develop a police force with artificial people who could also act as impartial judges?"

"A two-for-one deal," the President mused, sounding impressed. "That would solve half of our money problems. Perhaps those human communities who are currently advertising for help would be willing to fund the development."

"You can't manufacture artificial people to do a job like that," Kelly pointed out. "They'd have to choose the work, and once their body mortgages are paid off, I don't imagine many would find living in backwaters and watching humans behaving badly all that interesting."

"Perhaps our friends at QuickU could create a personality enhancement for policing," President Beyer said. "I'll bring it up next time we have lunch together."

Four

"Why is it so dark?" Kelly asked, after the lift door slid shut behind them. "Do you think we're on the right deck?"

"Give your eyes a minute to adjust," Joe advised her. "Kids, don't go running off until we can see where we are. Beowulf? You're on point."

The Huravian hound lifted his right-rear leg and marked the location of the lift tube, just in case. His eyes didn't need time to adjust to the low light on the deck and he could see that they were in a wide-open space, with no corridors or walls. Aside from the giant spokes piercing the floor and ceiling at regular intervals, there was little nearby to break the monotony of the mossy growth that covered the deck like a soft blanket. He trotted off towards the only thing of interest he had identified, a minor hump in the moss.

"Can anybody see more than me?" Kelly asked. "I'm holding my hand in front of my face and I can barely make out my fingers."

"Have you shifted your sensory band to infrared?" Banger asked helpfully.

"Humans have a fixed visual spectrum," Joe explained to the young Stryx. "Rods and cones."

"How about echo location?" Banger suggested. "Lots of biologicals can navigate by sound. Libby just taught us about bats and dolphins in school."

"We haven't evolved to that point yet," Joe said. "Any other ideas?"

"I think you'll have enough light to see in nineteen or twenty minutes," Banger replied. "The ceiling luminosity has increased by eleven percent since we entered."

"Maybe it's dawn," Kelly said. "We did start out a bit earlier than scheduled."

"Look, Mommy," Dorothy exclaimed, pointing in the direction Beowulf had taken. Everywhere the giant dog had stepped and crushed the moss, an eerie orange light had begun to glow, getting stronger by the second.

"There are some more lights off to the right," Joe said. "They aren't spaced right for Beowulf, though. Did somebody bring a ghost dog along?"

"Look at me," Samuel shouted, jumping up and down. "I made footprints that light up too!"

"I thought I told you to stay put," his father said in exasperation. The boy's figure was slowly illuminated in the bright spot he created by crushing more moss under his leaps. "I suppose those prints from your hind paws are actually Ailia's?"

"Yes, Mr. McAllister," the Vergallian girl called from the darkness. "You told us to stay together."

The ambient light increased as Dorothy and Mist scuffed their feet on the ground, allowing Kelly and Joe to exchange a parental look.

"Well, you have to admit it's different," Joe said. "The campsite is supposed to be near a waterfall, right? We may as well find our way there and set up camp, and afterwards we can see about exploring."

"I know where it is," Banger offered, spinning around in the air.

"Great, we'll follow you," Kelly said.

"But I can't show you," Banger added mournfully. "Libby made me promise not to."

"Samuel, Ailia," Joe called. "We're going to follow Beowulf and see if he can find the waterfall. Get over here now before you fall into a black hole or something."

Two sets of glowing footsteps angled to intercept the three brighter sets that were following in the giant dog's illuminated paw prints. Kelly suddenly flashed back to a Halloween party she had attended as a girl, where the children were given glowing tubes to navigate a haunted house. She flinched at the memory of a plastic skeleton dropping down in front of her from the ceiling. She remembered being terrified, but it was the sort of thing Dorothy would enjoy. Mist and Samuel too, though Ailia would probably faint.

"How about it, Killer?" Joe asked when they reached the dog, who had ultimately decided that the mossy mound was just the right height for a pillow. "Can you hear a waterfall?"

Beowulf wasted a long-suffering expression on the humans who couldn't make out his face, then rose to his feet and trotted off in a straight line towards the faint sound of falling water. Dorothy, Mist and Kelly immediately set out after him, following in his glowing steps, but Joe and Banger remained behind to wait for the smaller children to catch up.

"You can't just run off like that, especially in the dark," Joe lectured the pair of six-year-olds, though he was really talking to his son.

"We were just 'sploring," Samuel protested, kicking at the moss. "That's our job, isn't it? I'm hungry. Can I have some emergency rations now?"

"Is it an emergency?" Joe asked sternly.

"Yes. We're starving," Samuel insisted

Joe worked one arm out of a strap to let his backpack swing free from the other shoulder and opened a side pocket. He removed a handful of snacks, straining his eyes in the dim glow from the trampled moss to pick out a fruit bar, since the Vergallian girl couldn't tolerate chocolate or milk. He gave the appropriate bar to each child and shouldered the pack again.

"Thank you," Ailia said, peeling the wrapper back from her treat as she walked, nibbling on the end.

"That was good," Samuel added a few minutes later.

"Did you remember to save the wrapper or did you drop it?" Joe asked.

"I saved it," Samuel replied after a moment's hesitation.

Glancing over his shoulder, Joe saw a set of glowing footsteps racing backwards, so he stopped again to wait for the boy to find the wrapper and return. Ailia pressed a neatly folded square of paper and foil in his hand.

"You can see well in the dark?" Joe asked the girl in Vergallian.

"Pretty well," she replied. "It's not really dark with all of the glowing footprints."

"It is for us," Joe told her, wondering if Vergallians lost their acute night vision as they aged. Maybe they all had the ability but they hid it from their mercenaries? He'd have to remember to check with Woojin.

"Why are you guys dawdling along back there?" Kelly called. She had found herself alone after Dorothy and Mist pushed Beowulf to go faster, and she wasn't going to try keeping up with teenagers running in the near-dark.

"Just taking in the sights," Joe hollered back. "We're on vacation, you know."

Kelly waited until Joe and the children caught up, and then the five of them set off after the glowing footprints, Banger ostentatiously bringing up the rear where nobody could accuse him of interfering. Looking back the way they had come, Kelly saw that their tracks were fading, but there seemed to be a dim haze around the curved ceiling.

"I think the lights are beginning to brighten up," Kelly said.

"And something is starting to wake up," Joe replied. "Do you hear that?"

After the first few whistles and chirps, the birdsong quickly swelled in volume to become cacophonous. The light increased at the same pace, and soon they caught up with Beowulf and the girls, who had halted at the edge of a marsh.

"Beowulf can't hear the waterfall over the noise," Dorothy told them, practically shouting to make herself heard. "How come the birds here are so much noisier than on the ag deck?"

"I think there are a lot more of them," Kelly replied. "I wonder what they eat?"

Joe crouched down and turned over some damp soil, exposing a number of wriggling red worms. "Looks like there's a whole ecosystem supported in here," he commented. "I hope there aren't too many biting insects."

"Look, there's a grassy path right through all of the reeds," Dorothy said.

"Green grass," Joe observed. "When I was your age, my father told me that's the real dividing line between night and day, when you can start discerning colors."

"The path seems to be continuing in the direction Beowulf was heading before the birds starting singing," Kelly said. "Why don't we keep going for now and see where it leads?"

The marshy strip continued for about fifteen minutes of walking, all of it along the curvature of the deck. Eventually they emerged into an area crisscrossed with small streams which were bridged at regular intervals by metal ramps. They couldn't tell how deep the water was because it was covered by a dense mat of floating plants.

After closely observing the surface of one stream from a low metal crossing, Samuel declared, "The plants are blowing bubbles." Sure enough, when the others looked, they saw that small bubbles were breaking the surface between the crowded plants at regular intervals.

"The bubbles smell funny," Mist said, wrinkling her nose.

"Methane," Joe explained. "Could be all kinds of old plant matter decomposing in the stream bed."

"The spacing is too even," Dorothy said confidently. "It must be built that way."

"My little engineer," Kelly whispered to Joe. "It seems like just yesterday she thought everything happened because of magic."

Beowulf whined impatiently and pointed with a paw.

"I hear the waterfall!" Ailia declared. The avian orchestra had dialed back its performance, and the dull roar of water could be heard over the trills and whistles of the aspiring soloists.

"Let's get going then," Joe said, and the dog bounded off, the children and Banger chasing after him. The adults followed at a more sedate pace.

"I think the water is getting clearer," Kelly said. They crossed the largest stream yet, one which wasn't densely

42

matted with floating plant life. "Oh, and look at all of the fish."

"I wonder what makes the water flow," Joe mused. "It was barely moving at all back in the marsh. I'll bet the Stryx manipulate it with fields, and beneath the water's surface, they're running invisible paddle wheels of force that operate on the molecular level."

"It seems like an awful lot of effort to go to for a deck that nobody uses," Kelly said. "Maybe they keep it going for the birds and the fish."

"Libby said that we would be the first humans to visit this section, right?" Joe asked. "But all of this vegetation looks like it's from Earth, and even though the birds are avoiding us, I'm pretty sure I recognize their calls. This could be one of those decks they keep in reserve for emergencies."

"If it's an emergency deck, that calls for a chocolate bar," Kelly suggested hopefully. Joe shook his head in mock despair at the poor discipline of his troops in regards to their survival rations, but he dug in his pack and handed one over, not neglecting to help himself at the same time.

"Hey, we better speed up," Joe said after they finished their snack. "Beowulf just vanished into the ceiling, and the kids aren't far behind."

Kelly reluctantly stayed alongside her husband as he broke into a slow jog. They passed over a band of brilliant white sand, marred only by the tracks of the visitors. Before she had a chance to begin panting, the waterfall came into view and Joe slowed to a walk again.

"It's beautiful," Kelly exclaimed, her face lighting up with pleasure. "Look at all of the flowers. It's like some kind of tropical paradise."

"I'm finally going to get a chance to teach the boy how to swim," Joe said with satisfaction. "Ailia too, unless Vergallians hate going in the water. I don't remember."

"Are you sure the water will be safe?"

"Libby wouldn't have let us in here if it wasn't. And Banger can tell us if the water isn't clean, unless it's part of some Stryx secret."

"What's that the children are all looking at? Is it a hologram or a real old-fashioned display case?"

"It's a hologram. I can see that it's moving and it's really holding their attention. Even Beowulf is watching, and he usually ignores those things."

The roar of the waterfall prevented Kelly and Joe from hearing whatever audio went along with the hologram, and as soon as they were almost near enough to start making out details in the animated presentation, it vanished.

"Mommy, Daddy," Samuel shouted, running towards them. Suddenly, Banger got in front of the boy and seemed to be arguing with him.

As they approach the pair, Kelly heard the little Stryx telling Samuel, "But you promised, cross your heart and hope to turn into a Horten if you tell."

"What is it?" Kelly asked, crouching in front of her suddenly silent son.

"I can't," Samuel said, almost tearfully. "Don't want to be a Horten."

"Let the boy keep his word," Joe told Kelly, pushing Samuel off in the direction of Ailia. "He has to learn sometime."

"It's really cool," Dorothy said, coming up to them. "The presentation is on an automatic timer, it starts every fifteen minutes."

"How could you hear anything over the waterfall?" Kelly asked loudly.

"There's an acoustic barrier," Dorothy explained. "Around the campsite too, though it lets some of the sound through. Can we set up our tents now?"

"Alright," Joe said, lowering his pack to the ground. "You and Mist picked the red one, right?"

"White," Dorothy corrected him, no longer surprised at her father's inability to remember such important details.

Joe rooted around the main compartment of the pack and pulled out a small white sack, about the size of a loaf of bread.

"Here you go," he said. "I'll inflate the sleeping bags later."

Dorothy took the sack, nodded to Mist, and the two girls headed off to the far edge of the campsite, which was plainly delineated by a circle of white stones. The whole area had the rugged look of a wildlife sanctuary, but the absence of trees made it seem more like the seashore.

"Your turn," Dorothy said to Mist. "I set it up in practice."

Mist took the sack from her friend, opened it, and pulled out the intricately folded tent, a Sharf product that Peter Hadad recommended. The clone flipped through the folds looking for the trigger mechanism and activated it.

The tent began to unfold itself while still in Mist's hands. She squealed in delight as it rapidly grew in diameter until she couldn't hold it anymore, at which point it practically leapt away from her to land on the ground. The liquid crystals in the hemispherical tent ribs continued to slowly align themselves with the current from the micro-battery, and before five minutes had passed, the tent was fully deployed and ready for occupation.

"Didn't tents when we were kids have carbon fiber poles and stakes?" Kelly asked Joe. "I remember going on fishing trips with my dad, and it was a job to set it up."

"We had a real old-fashioned family-size tent when I was a kid," Joe replied. "Canvas with aluminum poles. The tent was too heavy for backpacking, and the poles were too awkward to carry far, even though they telescoped down to shorter lengths. You basically needed a canoe or a horse to carry the thing."

"Didn't your family have a car?" Kelly asked.

"Pick-up truck," Joe replied. "But we didn't take it camping."

"The hologram is about to start," Samuel interrupted urgently, pointing towards the presentation site. Joe and Kelly dutifully headed over to view it, lest the strain of keeping the contents secret caused the boy to explode. Their son led them into the little theatre, really just a few large blocks of stone arranged in a semi-circle around an unobtrusive projection unit. The sounds of the waterfall vanished as they stepped through the acoustic barrier, and the holographic digits began counting down to zero.

"Welcome to the Wetlands Machine," a pleasant voice stated. "Give us ten minutes and we'll give you clean water."

Ten minutes later, Kelly turned to Joe, feeling slightly queasy.

"Did you know that we were hiking through a wastewater treatment facility?" she asked.

"The thought occurred to me when we crossed the sand barrier after the big marshy area and the water flow picked up, but I didn't want to ruin the surprise. You have to hand it to the Stryx for building such a beautiful recycling system when they could have done it all with chemicals and radiation."

"But this is our drinking water!" Kelly protested.

"That's why the sign says to shower before swimming in the lagoon," Joe pointed out. "I wonder where the showers are?"

"Were you surprised, Mommy?" Samuel demanded. "Dorothy said she guessed when Mist said the air bubbles smelled funny."

"Your sister is a smart young woman," Kelly replied. "What are you staring at?"

"Beowulf," her boy replied. Kelly looked over and saw that the hound was standing up, pointing at the waterfall with a paw as if he'd spotted a bird in the brush. A minute later, a sopping wet couple appeared from behind the rushing water.

"Where's Ailia?" Aisha asked, as soon as they approached to within speaking distance. "Why isn't she with Samuel?"

"Me, Ailia and Banger are playing hide-and-seek," Samuel replied, looking guilty. "I was supposed to find them, but..."

"Crazy place to put a lift tube," Paul said, squeezing the water out of his shirt. "Libby sends her greetings and said to tell you that the bathrooms are behind the big red rock. I guess she means that one. She's been scrambling to finish off the accommodations before you arrived, but the bot who was supposed to put up that sign got distracted by the fish and dropped it into the lagoon."

Five

"My name is Walter Dunkirk, and I want to welcome you all to the first public meeting of the Human Expatriates Election League on Union Station. HEEL is a galaxy-wide movement established to promote human self-government and democracy, and I've been sent by headquarters to get the ball rolling in this sector. I'm sure you have a lot of questions, so rather than me standing up here and pretending to understand all of your local concerns, I'd like to start by going around the room and hearing from each and every one of you. But I'm not here to make decisions for you, so let's vote through a show of hands. All in favor?"

"He's good," Daniel murmured to Shaina, even as he raised a hand. "What? You aren't in favor of everybody saying something?"

"I've lived on this station my whole life," Shaina replied. "If there's a complaint I haven't heard, it's not worth hearing."

"That's nine in favor," Walter said. "All opposed?"

Shaina held up both of her hands, one of them behind Daniel's shoulder in an attempt to make it pass as his vote.

"That's two opposed, though the gentleman in the white shirt appears to have three arms," the political organizer observed, raising an eyebrow. "I'm glad you've decided in favor because I anticipate this group becoming

48

the core of a larger movement and it's important we get to know each other. May I ask if your objection is to public speaking or to having to listen to the others?" he continued, looking directly at Shaina.

"Both," she replied. "I've been to a dozen stations on business this year and I never heard of HEEL, so I came to learn something about it. If I'm going to sit around listening to local people complaining, I'd rather do it at night, in a bar, with drinks."

"Well, I'm still glad you're here since you make up ten percent of the audience," Walter replied. "I realize I could have done a better job promoting this meeting, but I have to admit being a bit surprised by the light turnout. Could I get you to say something about yourself since we've already broken the ice?"

"I'm Shaina Hadad," she replied grudgingly. "I'm in business with a Stryx partner and I'm perfectly happy with the current state of affairs on the station. I'm here to see whether or not I should be worried that your HEEL is going to screw it all up."

"Well, that's a refreshing viewpoint," Walter said, not in the least taken aback. "Maybe your attendance today will prove to be your first step on the road to Damascus. As long as we're starting with the naysayers, why don't you go next, Daniel. In the interest of full disclosure, I should state that I met Daniel in the Little Apple soon after I arrived on Union Station. When I decided against visiting him at the EarthCent embassy where he works, he suggested this café for a public meeting. Daniel?"

The junior consul rose from his seat and faced the little knot of station residents gathered in the café. Of the ten people at the meeting, five of them were there because Daniel had invited them. He was also surprised by the low attendance, given the number of corridor display ads HEEL had purchased. But Sunday morning was probably a bad time for political meetings since the rabble-rousers were home nursing hangovers.

"I'm Daniel Cohan, and I started as junior consul on the station a month ago, so I haven't really had time to fully assess the local conditions. Well, I could tell you a lot about the tables in the casino, but I don't suppose you're here for that. I'm in favor of democracy on general principle, though I've never actually voted, and I wouldn't complain if the Stryx promoted me to president one day."

"Thank you, Daniel. I can see I have my work cut out for me with this crowd," Walter said in his relaxed manner. "How about the young man with the skull tattooed on his face?"

"I'm, like, this isn't a new game?" the kid asked. "I thought it was, like, recruiting. Like FightOn did for their new Human Expatriates Piracy League game last year."

"Do you know what an election is?" Walter inquired.

"I thought it was, like, fighting, like," the young man replied. "There's a campaign, yeah?"

"You could view elections as a sort of a war, but our weapons are petitions and ballots."

"Excuse me," the kid said. "I just remembered I have to be somewhere." As he scraped back his chair and rose, another young man at a different table also stood up and followed.

"It's turning into quite a cozy meeting," Walter observed, seemingly unperturbed by his shrinking audience. "Perhaps we can hold the next one in my apartment. How about the young lady with the unique hat?"

"I'm Chance," she said, smiling flirtatiously at the HEEL organizer. "I heard about your meeting from Daniel, and he said you'd be taking suggestions for a unified platform. As long as you plan to break with the Stryx and everything, I want to make sure that you put cancellation of body mortgages on the list of demands."

"Body mortgages?" Walter asked.

"For artificial people, like me."

"Uh, I'm not sure artificial people are humans," Walter replied slowly. "I'll have to check with headquarters and see."

"Not humans?" Chance asked incredulously. "You just lost my vote, mister. Come on, Thomas."

Chance flounced out of the café and Thomas reluctantly followed her, casting an apologetic look back at Daniel.

"And then there were six," Walter said. He tried his best to sound jovial, but the strain of his rapidly diminishing audience was beginning to show around the corners of his mouth. "Who's next?"

"I'll go," said an elderly woman, whose hair was done up in a grey bun. "I'm Sylvia Garcia, and I voted in every election in Texas before my husband and I emigrated in our thirties. I don't remember much about it, other than the fact we would get a booklet from the League of Women Voters each year explaining what the ballot questions meant. I came because you're also a league, and I thought you could tell me if they're finally accepting men."

"Glad to have you, Sylvia," Walter replied. "I'm not aware of any connection between HEEL and the group you mentioned, but I'll make a note to check. As somebody who was an active participant in the democratic process, do you have any comments about the form of government here on the station?"

"I once saw our ambassador sitting on a throne made of skulls during a parade and she looked very uncomfortable.

51

I've never needed to go to the embassy for anything myself, so I can't say I have any complaints."

"Thank you. Next?"

"Henri Durand," declared a middle-aged man who wore a red beret. He rose from his seat, placed his right hand in his vest, and gave the end of his mustache a twist with his left. "There comes a time in every man's life that he is called upon to do great things. I believe that this is my time, our time, and we can do these great things together. I pledge my life and fortune to the cause!"

"Splendid, splendid," Walter said, but he seemed to be eyeing the man warily. "You haven't gone and, uh, done anything already, have you?"

"On the station?" Henri inquired in a suddenly subdued voice. "Are you crazy? The Stryx know everything that goes on here."

"That's what I'd heard," the HEEL organizer replied. "So, who's left?"

"Liza Brown," said a sad-looking woman. She was dressed in a baggy garment that appeared to be a sack with holes cut out for the arms and head. "I'm here to represent the Free Corridor Commune."

"I haven't heard of your group," Daniel said, turning in his chair to face the woman. "But I know that our embassy sponsors a take-it-or-leave-it center on the Shuk deck if you're down on your luck and you need something to wear."

"I'm a nudist," Liza said, too lethargic to bristle at his implied criticism of her attire. "Sunday mornings we play volleyball, but I drew the short straw and got stuck coming here to show our support or whatever."

"Or whatever," Walter repeated, sounding a little deflated. "That just leaves the scary gentleman in the back?"

"Clive Oxford. I'm the director of EarthCent Intelligence and I thought I should stop by to make sure you aren't planning on throwing any bombs. It's a good thing I came since you already chased away two of my best agents by questioning their human credentials."

"Oh. Pleased to make your acquaintance, Mr. Oxford. I'm rather new at this, you see, and I just didn't want to give the young, er, lady, an answer today that I'd have to reverse myself on tomorrow. I'm just a contract employee, really."

"Not a volunteer?" Daniel asked.

"Volunteer?" Walter looked surprised for the first time. "Who would do this sort of thing for free? I recently graduated with my PhD in Public Policy from the Kennedy School of Government, but I couldn't find any work on Earth. I got this community organizer job by responding to an ad that came through our alumni board. HEEL was seeking candidates with a deep knowledge of government who were willing to travel and do grassroots organizing."

"Should we recognize the Kennedy thing?" Clive asked.

"It's part of Harvard," Walter said.

"I think I've heard of that," Sylvia exclaimed, raising her hand. "It's in New Haven, right?"

"That's Yale," the public policy scholar replied with a sigh. "HEEL offered salary and expenses, so I thought I'd give it a try. Twenty straight years in school should qualify me for something, shouldn't it? I don't officially start until my materials arrive, but I thought, I'm here, so I may as well hit the ground running."

"You seem like a sharp enough guy to me," Daniel said, sensing that the meeting had devolved into a casual discussion. "What was all that business about the tyranny

53

of the unelected and the Stryx overlords you were spouting in the Little Apple?"

"Well, it's true, isn't it?" Walter countered. "I've never been off of Earth before, but everybody knows that the consolidated continental governments that arose after the Stryx invasion are the only true human democracies."

"Wait a minute," Shaina interrupted, jumping to her feet in agitation. "The Stryx invasion?"

"I don't know what else you could call it," the recently minted PhD countered. "Nobody invited them. They just took over our airwaves and networks, broadcast a bunch of propaganda about joining the galactic community, and then helped the other aliens introduce the largest labor exchange in history. How much of Earth's population sold itself into virtual slavery before the Stryx even got around to providing space elevators—on credit, if I may add."

"Earth would have torn itself apart if the Stryx hadn't stepped in," Shaina protested.

"That's their story," Walter retorted. "According to the textbooks, the world economy was on the brink of a recovery when the Stryx intervened. Our governments were nearing an agreement to introduce a new international currency backed by positive thinking, or maybe it was a tax on thinking, I don't recall the details. We didn't spend that much time on recent history, and my own research was on the successful adoption of a Marxism variant by semi-tropical citrus growers in the early years of the twentieth century."

"So you think the Stryx were just waiting for an excuse to swoop in and take over Earth because humans make such good unskilled labor?" Shaina asked sarcastically.

"My HEEL recruiter warned me that the station humans would be completely brainwashed by this point, but that's what you expect with asymmetric power relationships. It's the old Stockholm Syndrome in action."

"Now you look, Mister Citrus Growers," Shaina responded angrily. "I might not have spent half as much time in school as you, and I don't know anything about your syndromes and whatnot, but I know that I'm nobody's slave. How dare you come in here and talk down to us? I'll bet everybody in attendance has contributed more to humanity than you with your fancy education, and that includes the kid with the skull on his face who came by mistake."

"I'm sorry if I've upset you," Walter said, sounding truly apologetic. "It appears that my experience with student teaching and speaking in symposiums isn't translating to the public square as well as I'd hoped. I'm sure I have much more to learn from all of you than you have to learn from me. Can we start again from the beginning?"

Shaina was so surprised by the man's rapid retreat that she sat back down and nodded.

"I'm primarily interested in hearing about your HEEL organization," Clive said. "EarthCent is looking into helping humans who are setting up governments on some of the open worlds where we're beginning to see requests for policing. Perhaps we could work together."

"Didn't you say you're an EarthCent spy?"

"Head spy and bottle washer."

"And you don't see a problem in working with a movement whose ultimate goal is to replace EarthCent?"

"I think that's the ultimate goal for all of us, though we don't expect it to happen for a few hundred years," Clive replied calmly.

"So you think we should wait for the Stryx to tell us that we're ready to cast off their yoke?"

"Maybe they're waiting for us to tell them that we're ready," Clive replied. "We're not, if you were going to ask. Living as part of the tunnel network is a bit like living in a zoo, but in place of cages, the Stryx enforce some rules about interspecies relations. To extend the zoo analogy, we're one of the grazers, the kind without horns or anything."

"Zebras," Daniel suggested. "We're good at keeping our predators confused."

"I'm trying to understand you, but your concept of liberty clashes with everything I studied back on Earth." Walter sat down heavily in one of the chairs, looking physically drained. "I realize that the academic environment may have turned me into something of a hothouse flower, but surely the concepts of freedom and liberty are universal."

"Let me tell you about that since I'm here," Liza spoke up unexpectedly, coming out of her torpor. "The Free Corridor Commune didn't start off as a segregated group. Our goal was to bring freedom from clothing to all of the humans on the station. Given the advanced climate control on the human decks, clothing is no longer needed for warmth or protection from the sun and the weather. Some of the advanced species haven't worn clothing in millions of years."

"Like the Grenouthians," Daniel interjected.

"So around twenty years ago, a group of us decided to stop wearing our clothes, and we were sure the rest of the humans on the station would follow our lead. It didn't work that way. Some people stared at our bodies, some people wouldn't look at us at all, and then there was the groping in crowds." Liza stopped for a moment and shuddered. "But the worst part was the parents getting angry with us. They said we were infringing on their right to bring up their children without having to look at a bunch of—well, we learned that we don't all have the same ideas of freedom."

"So eventually you reached a compromise by creating a section exclusively for nudists," Walter summarized. "That's the classic solution, and a fine example of democracy in action."

"Actually, the Stryx station manager told us that the tenants were demanding action, and if we didn't want to put our clothes back on, we would either have to move or to pay for everybody else to move. It turned out that the small print in the Stryx leases includes a whole section about communal norms."

"I hadn't thought about the nudist thing in years," Shaina exclaimed. "I was only a girl, but I remember my father loaning a towel to a naked woman who came to the Shuk during the rush, when the crowds are so thick that we still get the occasional pickpocket."

"Thank you for sharing," Walter said, nodding to both women. "I'm beginning to see that life on a Stryx station follows a different pattern than I've been led to believe.

"So what can you tell us about HEEL?" Clive asked, persisting with his original inquiry. "What was the training course like? Did you meet any other new hires?"

"We didn't exactly have a training course and I haven't met any other organizers," Walter admitted. "I haven't even met my direct superior, except by holo-conference, of course. I'll know more about it when my materials get here. I've just been trying to make good use of my time until then."

"So all you really know about HEEL is that they placed an ad on your alumni board and have promised you a salary and materials that are due any day?"

"I did get a travel allowance and an advertising budget," Walter said. "You don't think I'd come all the way out here on my own creds?"

"Well, I hope you'll stop by our offices when your materials show up," Clive told Walter. "Even if we can't work together, I see no reason we should find ourselves on opposite sides.

"I'm curious too," Daniel said. "Hey, where did Henri go?"

"He snuck off after making his little speech about shared sacrifice," Sylvia told them.

Six

"Hurry up, they're expecting us for dinner," Lynx called up to Woojin, who hadn't followed her down the Prudence's ramp. "We're supposed to present an image of good governance to these people and I don't want to start by being late. You're just as bad as Thomas."

"You try shaving during reentry on a two-man trader sometime," Woojin called back. "I almost cut my own throat. If you didn't have that tube of Farling skin-knit in the first-aid kit, you might have been a widow before I had the chance to place a life expectancy bet with the Thark bookmakers."

"Some mercenary hero you are," she yelled irritably. "Just put on a clean shirt and hurry up. We hit the ground running in this outfit."

"Yes, Ma'am!" Woojin responded, as if they were on a parade ground. A minute later he emerged from the hold tucking his shirt into matching black pants. "But if you're going to bring up your old boyfriends every time I shave, it's going to be a long marriage."

"Are those the best clothes you brought?" she asked, eyeing the mercenary dress uniform critically.

"I've got two more sets in black."

"But those are—never mind." She issued a silent in-struction over her implant to the ship's controller to raise

59

the ramp which doubled as the main hatch for the Prudence's hold.

"Here comes our transportation," Woojin said, pointing with his smoothly shaven chin to indicate an approaching dust trail. "That's a Dolly floater they're driving, and I'll be glad of the ride after a week in Zero-G. Did you really spend ten years in that tin can?"

"Hard to believe it now," Lynx replied. She did a deep knee-bend to see if her joints would be making embarrassing cracking noises now that her body weighed something again. Fortunately, gravity on the open world of Chianga was barely two-thirds of Earth standard, as the towering Dollnicks preferentially focused on terraforming worlds that didn't give them backaches and flat feet. "You killed my old record on the tie-down treadmill," she added grudgingly.

"Running the recruits around Mac's Bones keeps me in shape. I wonder how Thomas is doing with the new group. He didn't seem very enthusiastic about following the basic training program Joe and I developed."

"Now who's bringing up my old boyfriends?" Lynx asked playfully. She licked her index finger and chalked a mark on an invisible blackboard. "Besides, you're the one who jumped at Blythe's offer to pay for the honeymoon in return for stopping by a few of the human settlements that were advertising for cops. We'll be lucky if we only spend three out of the four weeks on my ship."

"And you're the one who's been talking about getting her ship out of mothballs ever since we met. Besides, given our age difference, I thought I'd make a better impression in Zero-G."

"I'm just saying, if everything goes wrong and we have to eat worms or something, it's your fault."

"Are we having our first argument?"

"What are you talking about?" Lynx retorted. "We argue all of the time."

A barely audible hum announced the arrival of the floater, which came to a hovering stop just in front of the recently arrived visitors. A young boy wearing a sort of a sun-helmet sat at the controls, and a girl who looked like his sister occupied the other front seat. The Dollnick floater resembled a spaceport courtesy transport with four rows of seats and no visible means of propulsion.

"Climb in," the girl told them. "If we set down in the sand too often the filters will get clogged."

Lynx swung a leg over the edge of the craft and then accepted a boost from Woojin, who followed by vaulting into the next row back. The floater dipped alarmingly at his sudden entry, but then recovered. He clambered over the low seat-back to join Lynx in the row behind their young drivers.

"I'm Sephia and he's Raythem," the girl told them. The floater spun about on the spot and began to accelerate rapidly. A lack of wind in their faces showed that the craft employed some type of force field technology, without which conversation would also have been impossible. "You're the first people from Union Station who have ever come to visit us. We know all about your home from LMF. It's my favorite show."

"I'm Lynx and he's Woojin. I'll make sure to tell Aisha that you watch."

"I haven't watched that show in two years," the boy said haughtily, lest they get the wrong idea. "It's for little kids."

61

"You know Aisha?" Sephia asked, wide-eyed in astonishment. "Dianna says that she's just a hologram created by artificial intelligence. Nobody could really be that nice."

"I eat with Aisha all the time so you can tell Dianna that she's wrong," Lynx replied. "How old are you two?"

"I'm seven, and Raythem's ten," Sephia said. "Daddy only lets him drive the floater if I come because Raythem knows I'll tell on him if he goes too fast."

"I'm a good driver," Raythem asserted.

"I didn't know the Dollnicks made floaters sized for humans," Woojin said. "The ones I've seen were more than twice as big as this one."

"We make them in our own factory, with Dollnick parts," the boy explained without looking over his shoulder. "Daddy says that people who won't use alien technology are just dumb."

"I guess I can agree with your father there," Lynx replied. "Is that dome up ahead your town?"

"That's the factory," the girl said. "Daddy says the dome keeps out all of the dust, and when we visit, we have to go through a little room where the walls blow on us. Then we have to put on plastic clothes over our real clothes. Everybody inside looks really funny. What do they call it, Ray?"

"A clean-room," the boy replied. "Daddy says it's because the Dollnick parts are so small and fit so close together that a bit of dust you can't even see could ruin a floater drive unit."

The floater raced past the dome and the sandy surface gave way to agricultural fields. At one point, they saw a group of humans in the distance working with what looked like a giant spool of black wire or pipe.

"Drip irrigation," Woojin commented. "They manage their water carefully on this world."

"Water is money," the little girl said reflexively, repeating something she must hear from adults all the time.

The floater began to slow as they came over a small rise, and a strange settlement sprang into view before them. The houses were all cookie-cutter prefab structures that looked like they had been delivered directly from a factory with only the slightest aesthetic modifications. Lynx counted more than twenty concentric circles of grassy streets before she gave up and asked the children, "What's that metallic tower in the middle?"

"It's our rock zapper," the girl told her without hesitation, since it was obvious that Lynx couldn't have been referring to anything else. "Sometimes it lights up at night to shoot meteors and stuff. It's real pretty, but it makes the air smell funny while it's working."

The boy slowed the floater to the speed of a galloping horse as they approached the outermost houses.

"Press the button," the girl told him.

"I did already," the boy replied, a little too quickly.

"Did not. I watched you. And the green light isn't on."

"But I know how to get there," Raythem protested.

"I'll tell Daddy," Sephia warned him.

"Alright, alright," the boy said, pushing the autopilot button. The floater immediately sped up, but Lynx relaxed. She knew that kids on outposts and ag worlds learned how to operate equipment early, but that didn't mean she wanted a ten-year-old driving her through town traffic. The autopilot navigated too fast for her liking, but at least it had a built-in collision avoidance system, probably.

"Home," the boy said sullenly, after the floater came to a rather abrupt halt. It settled onto the grass, and the four occupants were able to exit easily by simply stepping over the gunwales. A deeply tanned man wearing shorts and a T-shirt waited for them.

"I'm Bob Winder," he introduced himself, at the same time tossing a coin to each of his children. They eagerly caught the money and ran off without saying where they were going. "I hope my son didn't scare you with his driving, but I thought it would be a more important use of my time to talk a couple of other mayors into coming. They should be arriving any minute."

"I'm Pyun Woojin and this is my wife, Lynx. Please call me Wooj." The two men shook hands.

"Lynx Edgehouse," Lynx said, shaking Bob's hand.

"You're married but you use different names?" Bob asked.

"I'm keeping my options open, just in case," Lynx replied. "Thank you for agreeing to meet with us on such short notice. We were originally planning to contact you from at least a day out, but the tunnel controller dumped us in such a low orbit that landing immediately was the only thing that made sense."

"The Dollnicks prefer it that way," Bob said. He ushered them into the house through an odd double-door and led them into a sunken living room, indicating that they should seat themselves. "Very efficient people, might have something to do with the four arms. Of course, I've never been off Chianga myself, so I'm not familiar with planetary approach methodologies."

"You were born here, Mayor?" Lynx inquired.

"Born and raised," the mayor responded proudly. "My parents came out in the first wave from Earth and never went back. I grew up on the main continent, but when the Dollnicks declared Chianga an open world and offered financing to humans willing to colonize the outlying land masses, I signed up immediately."

"You've certainly done a lot in a short time," Woojin said, looking around the well-appointed home. "Are these structures manufactured by the Dollnicks?"

"Everything you see in my home was made by human hands, though we use a lot of Dollnick equipment in the factories," Bob said. "The mayor of Houses will be here tonight, so you can ask her about the process yourself."

"You named a town Houses?" Lynx asked.

"All of our towns are named for their factories," the mayor replied, making it sound like the only logical possibility. "Is there some other way of doing it?"

"On Earth, cities and towns are named after local geological features, or the place the settlers came from, or for the people themselves," Lynx said. "In fact, the two times I visited Earth, it seemed that half of the places I went had a prefix, as if they ran out of ideas."

"Like New Houses, or West Houses, or North…"

"He gets the idea," Lynx interrupted her husband.

"Nope, makes no sense to me," Bob said, shaking his head. "We live in Floaters because the factory makes floaters. That's how the Dollnicks name their towns and it's good enough for us. But where are my manners?" he cut himself off and rose. "What can I get you to drink?"

"Anything distilled is fine by me," Woojin said.

"Make mine with plenty of water," Lynx added.

"Best water on Chianga comes from our deep wells," the mayor boasted. "You've made a wise choice."

There was a loud hiss and a skittering sound from the other room which made Lynx's hair stand up on the back of her neck. She turned to Woojin to see if he was preparing to fend off an attack of giant insects, but he looked completely relaxed.

"Could you trigger the door, Martha?" the mayor called. He turned back to his guests with a conspiratorial grin. "My wife is in the kitchen trying to make take-out look home-made. She commutes to Furniture, which is down south a ways, and she got home from work later than me today."

The front door opened and two women entered.

"So the two of you came in one floater," Bob commented. "What can I fix you for drinks?"

"You'd ask ME that question?" said the taller of the pair. She carried what appeared to be a doctor's bag, and when she pressed a hidden button on the handle, the sides flopped down, exposing a salesman's display of small liquor bottles. "I'm not one to waste a trip out of town just to talk politics. We've got some new products coming out, including a fair version of dark rum."

"I was about to tell our visitors that we don't stand on formality around here, so Wooj, Lynx, let me introduce you to my closest mayoral colleagues. The booze hound there is Terri, the mayor of Distilling, and her designated driver this evening is Sheila, the mayor of Houses.

"Great to meet you, Wooj, Lynx," the shorter woman said. "Let me have one of those Scotch samples, Terri, and that will be it for my evening. The last one you tried on me was the right color, but it tasted like medical alcohol mixed with tea."

"How many factory towns do you have on Chianga?" Woojin asked their host, accepting a short tumbler full of oily yellow liquid and passing on to Lynx a glass with a diluted version of the same.

"We're up to forty-seven now, and some of them are practically cities," Bob replied. "I could have invited a couple more mayors from the closer factories today, but I thought it made more sense to check you out first, if you don't mind my saying."

Lynx coughed, turned red, and spit her drink back out into her glass. The mayor of Distilling leapt up and pressed a sample bottle into her hands.

"Drink this," she ordered. "It's branch water, or at least, that's what we call it."

Lynx took the small bottle greedily, gargled, and swallowed.

"It's my fault," Woojin said to their host. "Lynx worked as an independent trader for ten years, so I just assumed she'd have developed a taste for Dollnick tequila."

"Try the Scotch," Sheila suggested. "It's a big improvement over the last batch."

"Don't everybody ruin their appetites," cautioned a black-haired woman as she maneuvered a service floater into the room. "Hi, girls," she said to the visiting mayors before introducing herself to the visitors from Union Station. "I'm Marge. Sorry I wasn't out earlier but I was busy in the kitchen. You must be Woojin and Lynx. I'm honored you made us the first stop on your honeymoon tour."

"Everything looks wonderful, Marge," Sheila said. "I don't know how you do it with your schedule."

"Yes, I'm dying for something to chew on," Lynx added, having recovered her voice. "We've been eating out of squeeze-tubes the last week."

"Get it while it's hot," Bob suggested in his hearty manner. "We won't have to worry about competition from the kids this evening. They're off spending their chauffeur earnings on a combination pizza with fungus and Sheezle bugs, no doubt."

"I wish you wouldn't encourage them," Martha reprimanded her husband. "I know the baked Sheezle bugs are a good source of calcium, and the insoluble fiber won't hurt them either, but some of the fungi make it impossible to get them in bed on time."

"You guys eat Sheezle bugs?" Lynx asked in astonishment.

"Mainly for the crunch," Sheila said. "Kind of like chocolate-covered ants."

Lynx had barely made a dent in her meal when Woojin polished off his first plateful and went for seconds. She hoped that Marge hadn't noticed how she was examining every forkful for signs of anything suspicious in the pasta sauce. Maybe she should make something up about food allergies?

"I see you know how to eat," the mayor of Floaters said to Woojin approvingly. "I was afraid you were going to be a repeat of the political organizer who came through last week. He started by telling us that it was his first time off of Earth, and then he asked if we could let him have a bit of water to add to some dehydrated junk he'd brought from the mother world."

"He worked for HEEL," Marge added helpfully.

"I've never met a HEEL agent myself, but I hear that one showed up on Union Station recently," Woojin said. He swallowed another forkful of the Italian/Dollnick fusion cuisine and smacked his lips in loud appreciation. "Supposedly they're popping up all over the tunnel network."

"That man talked the strangest mixture of sense and insanity I ever did hear," Marge said, watching out of the

68

corner of her eye as Lynx finally began eating like a normal person. "Self-government, self-sufficiency, earning our place amongst the advanced species, all things we believe in. But he kept bringing up how we have to break away from the Stryx and stop letting them run our lives. I've never met a Stryx and I wouldn't know one from any other AI if I did. But without their opening Earth, we'd probably all have killed each other by now, unless the Vergallians had moved in and taken over the planet."

"The HEEL guy showed up at our distillery dome last week asking if he could address the workers and hand out some informational holo-cubes," Terri said. "I gave him permission to talk in the cafeteria at lunch since we don't get much in the way of entertainment at work, unless your idea of a good show is watching our quality control tasters staggering around. He didn't say anything about the Stryx, but after talking about self-determination and holding free elections, he made some mysterious references to a Big Brother."

"Probably us," Woojin said, polishing off his second plate of pasta. "Are those spoon worms for eating, or did you just put them out for display?"

"Dessert," Marge informed him. "They're the closest we can come to Dollnick Snakees, which are unfortunately toxic to humans. We imported some starter worms from Earth and farm them in the salt marshes. You've cleaned your plate twice, so I guess you can go ahead of us."

"Have mine," Lynx muttered, looking rapidly away from the bowl of creepy-crawlies which she hadn't noticed previously.

"I grew up on these," Woojin said with a happy grin, adding a bit of salt to a worm before slurping it down. "You don't know what you're missing."

69

Lynx gagged on her linguini, which suddenly felt alive in her mouth. The Chiangans regarded her with a mixture of pity and amusement.

"Do you mind my asking if the two of you are undercover agents?" Terri inquired. "Bob just told us to expect a recently married Union Station couple from EarthCent, but the holo-cubes that HEEL man distributed included some pretty strong accusations about humans spying on humans and running a shadow government."

"That's us," Woojin told her cheerfully, ladling a generous dollop of spoon worms onto his plate where he dressed them with oil. "We aren't undercover though, or I'd have to kill you all. That's a joke," he added, when the other diners froze. "I haven't killed anybody in years."

"It's not very exciting," Lynx said, realizing she had better interrupt before Woojin's sense of humor dug them a hole they'd never get out of. "We're mainly focused on business intelligence to pay the bills. I'm actually the cultural attaché at the Union Station embassy, so maybe that's our shadow government."

"You're not here to help us organize elections, maybe put your own names in as candidates?" Shelia suggested playfully.

"We're really here on a fact-finding honeymoon," Woojin said, pausing to slurp up a choice morsel of spoon worm flesh. "I worked a couple of police assignments for aliens in my previous career so I'm supposed to be the expert."

"So you saw our advertisement for a part-time marshal, and even though you aren't getting into the business, you thought you'd like to see who was hiring," Bob summarized.

"We're still feeling our way forward," Woojin told him. "Most Earth expatriates live under alien control of one type or another, mainly business consortiums. The few truly independent human colonies we've visited in the past were able to scrape by without official governments, thanks to special circumstances. But with, what did you say, forty-seven factory towns and a growing need for policing, you seem to be moving towards a real government here."

"Not so fast," Terri said with a smile. "We have our own special circumstances as well. For starters, we currently don't accept any immigrants, so everybody in our towns grew up under the rule of Prince Drume. Although he doesn't exert any direct control over this continent, he holds all of the mortgages and grants all of the technology licenses. Our people know that if we held an election and established an Earth-style government, it wouldn't be able to do much differently than we're doing already."

"Aren't you elected?" Lynx asked.

"Sure, we're elected to run our factories," the mayor of Distilling replied. "The town belongs to the factory, of course, so we're stuck dealing with municipal issues as well. The factories hold an election once a year, that's about every five hundred days if you're still using the Earth calendar on Union Station, but the process is pretty informal. All of the tenured employees get together outside on a nice day, and the ones dumb enough to want to be mayor go and stand up front where everybody can see them. The people who want to vote for a particular candidate form a line behind that person. I've never heard of an election being so close that anybody had to count the people in the lines."

"Sounds like the same system the Dollys use on their private worlds," Woojin commented.

"Of course," Bob said. "If you can't beat 'em, join 'em, and we sure as heck can't beat 'em. I guess we've adopted everything we can from the Dollnicks, except for their sports, though some of the kids even fool around with artificial arm sets just to try. And it's no great privilege being mayor, if you were wondering. None of us have time for production work anymore, it's all management and inter-factory relations. I spend so much time visiting Library and Infrastructure that the neighbors are beginning to think I've moved out."

"You have a whole town dedicated to a library?" Lynx asked.

"They have a library, but the town handles education and recordkeeping as well," Sheila replied. "We use the same Stryx-supplied teacher bots as Earth because the price is unbeatable, but we also send our kids to Library two days a week, for classrooms with human teachers. They mainly follow the Dollnick curriculum."

"And Infrastructure handles your power, water, sewer and such?" Woojin asked.

"Infrastructure does the installation and maintenance, but the equipment is still leased from the Dollnicks," Bob replied. "You know the Dollnicks have been terraforming worlds for millions of years so they're experts at providing all of the utilities needed by biologicals. Our factories specialize in goods we can barter locally with the other towns or export for hard Nickies."

"So you're on the Dollnick currency base as well," Woojin said.

"Of course," Bob replied. "What else would we use?"

"Would you mind if we take a break to watch 'The Vanished Princess' on the holo?" Terri asked. "If I miss an episode, I won't have a clue what anybody is talking about at home or at work tomorrow."

"I'm sure our guests won't mind," Bob answered for them. He turned on the local version of a Dollnick holo projector, manufactured under license. "If you've never watched a Dolly serial, you're in for a treat. Best entertainment in the galaxy."

Seven

"Well, I have to admit that Libby was right not to tell us beforehand," Kelly said, as they all crowded into a lift tube after finishing off their lunch. "Who would have thought that a week in a waste water treatment facility could be so relaxing?"

"I wouldn't call it a facility," Joe objected. "They weren't even using pumps after all. The way the ground went right up near the ceiling behind the waterfall, they actually created enough elevation change on the deck for the water to flow through the filters. It's more of a natural machine."

"When I grow up, I want to be a toilet maker," Samuel announced.

"Everybody in?" Kelly asked, counting heads. "Where's Banger? Oh, there you are. Week Two of the McAllister vacation, please," she instructed the lift tube. The capsule accelerated smoothly, and the trip went on for much longer than the standard commute from Mac's Bones to the embassy or the Little Apple. Finally, the door slid open to reveal an eerie blue glow. Beowulf stuck out his head, sniffed, and then looked over his shoulder at Joe.

"Go ahead, boy," Joe told the dog. "Whatever it is, Libby wouldn't have sent us here if it ate oversized hounds with high self-esteem."

With that reassurance, Beowulf decided to put aside the spooky feeling the deck gave him and at least make a good show of it. He emerged into the strange blue light and the weird whispers, and then froze as a hand reached out of nowhere to touch his nose. It went right through his head, like when he walked into the middle of one of the holo-casts humans were so fond of, but that didn't make Beowulf any happier. He turned around to get back into the lift, but everybody had crowded out behind him and the door had already slid shut. The dog sat down on the deck and resolved not to budge.

"Are they all ghosts, Daddy?" Dorothy asked, sounding a little less sure of herself than usual. She and Mist each had a grip on the other's upper arm, and they stood pressed together, side-by-side.

"I don't know, Dot," her father replied, setting down his pack in case he needed to be free for action. "What do you think, Kel?"

"There's no such thing as ghosts," Kelly declared. She studied the disembodied forms for a clue as to their origin. "It's just some sort of holo display Libby has created for us, though why she chose such figures, I can't imagine."

They all halted for a moment, examining the densely packed array of translucent aliens, all floating at impractical angles between the deck and the ceiling. Kelly got the distinct feeling that the alien projections were somehow disappointed in the new arrivals for not being somebody else. The overall impression she got from the forms was that of smooth-bodied, long-tailed humanoids with oversized heads.

"Are the holo-things friendly?" Samuel asked Banger.

"They aren't holographic projections, they're energy matrices," the little Stryx told his friend. "I can do the math, but I don't know how to describe them to you."

75

"Can't you ask somebody?" Ailia suggested. She had only kept her eyes open long enough to find Samuel's hand, which she clenched tightly. The boy wasn't complaining and trying to shake free for a change.

"I just checked with Jeeves and he says they're ghosts," Banger replied.

Dorothy and Mist screamed, and Kelly was sure that the hair on the back of her neck was sticking up the same way as Beowulf's. "You know what a practical joker Jeeves is," she said uncertainly. "How can they be ghosts?"

"What's to worry about with things that can't even touch us?" Joe said. He jogged a few steps into the swarm of glowing beings, swinging his arms through dozens of apparitions as he went. "See? There's nothing to be afraid of."

"I don't like it," Kelly said, but she was already beginning to calm down. Ghosts or not, she had met plenty of strange aliens in the last thirty years, and whether they were technically alive or not didn't make that much difference. "Shouldn't there at least be a sign or something telling us where to go?"

"Follow the white arrows on the deck," intoned a disembodied voice.

Dorothy and Mist screamed again, pointing at various grotesque shapes which they imagined they had seen speak, and obviously enjoying themselves greatly. Joe looked around, squinting against the strange blue light that seemed to emanate from the ghosts. "Does anybody see an arrow on the deck?" he asked. Samuel got down on his hands and knees and began examining the deck minutely, forcing Ailia to crawl along with him since she wouldn't let go of his hand.

"Maybe the bot who was supposed to paint the arrow didn't get to it," Kelly suggested, recalling the lack of signage on the last deck.

"Did you see an arrow, boy?" Joe asked the giant dog. Beowulf shook his head in the negative, but Kelly thought she saw the tip of a white triangle sticking out from under furry ribs.

"I think he's lying on it, Joe," she said.

Beowulf gave the humans his "Who? Me?" act, and ostentatiously examined the deck to either side of his body before looking back at Joe and shaking his head.

"Come on, get up," Joe ordered. The dog rose grudgingly, giving Kelly a look that implied she was making preparations for her own funeral. A large white arrow was revealed, and it pointed right through the thickest section of spirits.

"They're moving away," Mist called excitedly.

"Like the Red Sea in the immersive," Dorothy added.

Sure enough, a passage through the packed ghosts was opening up along the direction the arrow pointed, and a bright light could be seen beyond. Whatever the apparitions consisted of, apparently they blocked light, even as they themselves glowed.

"Follow me," Joe said, shouldering the pack and heading into the open channel. "Beowulf, you can bring up the rear if you want."

As it turned out, Beowulf wanted to be right in the middle of the pack, behind Joe and the big girls. Kelly prodded Samuel and Ailia into the passage after the dog, and was grateful when Banger ushered her in next, taking the final place in line himself.

"They're all trying to talk at once," Ailia said, her thin voice barely audible in the wash of alien whispers. "Do you think they want something from us?"

"I can't imagine what we could give to ghosts," Kelly replied, finally accepting that the flitting and insubstantial bodies were in some way alive. "Let's just get through this passage and then we can have some emergency rations."

In a few short minutes, the press of ghosts began to thin out and a park-like landscape became visible through the remaining translucent bodies. Initially the view reminded Kelly of the works of the French Impressionists, but after another hundred steps, the scene snapped into such sharp focus that she might have been looking at a photograph. The manicured flora and delicate sculptures were so well defined that it was hard to believe they were real and not a doctored image.

"Aside from the unsettled spirits it's pretty nice," Joe declared, surveying the gardens. "I've seen some fancy royal parks on the Vergallian and Dollnick worlds, but this place takes the prize."

"Assuming the ghosts can't do any gardening, does that mean it grows this way, or is the work all done by bots?" Kelly asked.

"A new ghost is here, Daddy," Dorothy shrieked, pointing in excitement. "He looks almost human."

Before their eyes, the new apparition slowly solidified, and with the exception of the bald, oversized head, it did appear to be a standard humanoid. Even more startling, it was dressed in a tuxedo and patent leather shoes. Only the exposed skin of the hands and the head retained the ethereal appearance.

"Forgive me if I startled you," the ghost said. "I've taken the liberty of requesting the station manager to aid me in vocalizing the language native to four of your group and I hope the others will understand. May I ask if the big hairy one is your leader?"

Beowulf and Joe both puffed out their chests in acknowledgement.

"We don't have a leader," Kelly said. "We're on vacation. I'm Kelly, this is my husband Joe, our children Dorothy and Samuel, and their friends Mist, Ailia and Banger. The other hairy one is Beowulf."

"Ah, a formal introduction," the ghost replied. "My own name in our native system of communication has no vocal component, but perhaps you could call me Marvin."

"Are you friends with Libby?" Dorothy asked.

"Libby, Libby," the ghost mused. "You mean the station manager's young offspring who serves as the librarian? We spoke with her recently about opening our deck to visitors and I suppose you are the result. My comrades were no doubt expecting to greet a species we are familiar with, but you'll do."

"Do what?" Joe asked suspiciously.

"Why, enjoy our deck," Marvin replied, as if it was the most obvious thing in the world. "I have volunteered as tour guide, being the youngest of my kind, and I will be happy to answer any questions you might have."

"Are you really ghosts?" Samuel asked. Ailia shivered beside him.

"Ghosts, now there's a tricky concept. I can see how you might make the argument that it's the best description which your, shall we say, incompletely developed language can supply. If it makes you uncomfortable, I assure you that we are not dead in any sense of the word, other than having discarded our bodies. In fact, if being immortal is the opposite of being dead, we are about as undead as you can get."

"What did he say?" Samuel asked.

"They aren't REAL ghosts," Dorothy replied.

"Oh." Samuel sounded disappointed, but he turned back to Marvin and asked, "So what do you do?"

"Do?" The newly demoted ghost seemed taken aback by the question. "Why, we live, of course. Isn't it obvious?"

"Can you make anything happen?" Dorothy asked. "Like, do you keep these gardens so pretty and make new sculptures?"

"Ah, you like our sculptures," Marvin replied. "They're perfect, aren't they? One of the reasons we gave up corporeal existence was that we had done everything worth doing. The gardening is now in the hands of bots, of course. The station manager supplied new ones when the original equipment we brought to the station wore out around twenty million years ago."

"So you just fly around and haunt an empty deck all day?" Joe asked. It wasn't a very diplomatic way of putting the question and Kelly nudged him in the ribs with her elbow.

"Haunt?" Marvin sounded amused. "Wouldn't we need to have somebody here in order to haunt them?" He paused for a moment, assuming the pose of Rodin's famous statue. "I think therefore I am. Does that sound familiar? I borrowed it from one of your own primitive philosophers."

"For tens of millions of years?" Kelly asked in astonishment. "You and the rest of your race, you float around in here and think?"

"We aren't limited to just Union Station. My people have decks on several stations which are still maintained by the Stryx. It's not impossible that we still persist elsewhere as well, since the automated systems we created were as perfect as biological hands could make them. But then again, they did wear out here, didn't they? It's much more sensible to leave it to the AI in the end."

"I'm bored," Samuel declared. "Can I go exploring now?"

"Take Ailia and Banger and stay within sight," Joe said. "Dorothy, if you and Mist want to look around, bring Beowulf."

"Thanks, Daddy."

"Thank you, Mr. McAllister."

Kelly and Joe were left alone with the ghost, who seemed to have run out of things to say.

"I don't understand how anybody could abandon their bodies," Kelly remarked.

"It's easy when you're sufficiently advanced," Marvin replied. "It's merely a question of organizing your thoughts to the point that they defy entropy. Then you stop feeding the body, which you'll have come to see as a disgusting biological artifact, and all that remains behind is the mind."

"So what were the automated systems you perfected that the Stryx stand in for on the stations?" Joe asked.

"Just some necessary plumbing," Marvin replied, looking a little uncomfortable for the first time. "Without the aid of containment fields, thoughts in space tend to bleed over into each other, no matter how focused. The manifestations you saw earlier, and the projection of myself which is conversing with you now, are examples of containment fields."

"And the containment fields on this deck are supplied by the Stryx," Joe said.

"No. Yes. Well, in a manner of speaking," Marvin replied. "This field is created by my mentality, but through the intermediation of the station manager. A rough comparison might be humans creating music with instruments."

"The Stryx are your instruments?" Kelly asked skeptically.

"Perhaps that wasn't a good analogy," Marvin admitted. "It's more like the implants you carry in your heads. You ask for something, perhaps a fact from the station librarian, and you get the answer. The real creative work is in the asking. The rest is mere information retrieval and computation."

"We're going to walk around a bit," Joe said, cutting the conversation short. "Maybe we can talk more later."

"Certainly," Marvin replied. As the McAllisters walked away, the ghost called after them, "Don't forget to tell your Libby how cooperative I am."

Left alone by the ghosts, the family spent until suppertime exploring the extensive sculpture gardens in all their dizzying glory. There were small ponds with floating plants that blossomed at the approach of the visitors and folded up their flowers when the people moved on, as if admiration was their form of pollination. There were dwarf trees laden with surrealistic alien fruits, but when Samuel stretched for something that resembled a purple banana crossed with a pineapple, the branch lifted it out of his reach. There were dazzling creatures with gossamer wings flitting about, something between a butterfly and a hummingbird, and though they occasionally hovered for a few seconds in front of the visitors trespassing on their domain, none of them displayed any aggressive intentions.

"The last arrow we saw was pointing this way, and I don't see any other trees growing right up to the ceiling, so this must be the rendezvous point," Joe declared, setting down his pack on a stone bench. "I wonder what leftovers Ian will be sending along for our dinner tonight."

Kelly glanced at her decorative wristwatch and then checked the time against her implant to be sure. "We still have a few minutes to wait, and I'm not starting without the children."

"Banger will bring in Sam and Ailia on time," Joe said. "They were only one hedgerow to the left last time I checked, and I see them coming through the turnstile as we speak."

"I don't understand why they have turnstiles between the different gardens," Kelly complained. "It spoils the whole effect."

"Kind of like a museum or something," Joe agreed. "Maybe they want to count the visitors."

"I haven't seen Dorothy or Mist for a while. Aren't you going to whistle for Beowulf or something?"

"Something," Joe replied, removing from his pack a bag of pretzels delivered from the Just Like Home snacks store in the Little Apple.

"You think Beowulf can smell pretzels?"

"I won't even have to open them." Joe held the bag over his head and crinkled it once or twice. The sound created by the oriented polypropylene plastic was unique to the galaxy of human salty snack bags, and a moment later, Beowulf came bounding over a hedge that was taller than Kelly.

"Good ears, boy," Joe said. "Now what did you forget?"

Beowulf hung his head for a moment, and then took a running start to clear the hedge a second time and go back for the girls.

"Delivery," a voice called behind them. The McAllisters turned to see Clive and Blythe emerging from the fat tree trunk.

"Do you guys think you're elves or something?" Kelly asked. "Where are the twins?"

"With my mom," Blythe replied. "You didn't find the table?"

"Nice camouflage," Clive said, admiring the artificial tree they had arrived in. "I don't remember ever seeing a lift tube disguised like this before."

"Where's the food?" Joe asked.

"Oops," Clive said. He reached back into the capsule and pulled out a floating caterer's food chest emblazoned with the Pub Haggis artwork. "Ian pinged us this afternoon. He had a fancy Condolence Meal cancel, turned out the guy wasn't really dead, so he's been trying everybody he knows to take some of it off his hands. We made a deal with Libby to deliver in return for covering our share."

"I didn't realize that you were economizing," Kelly said.

"Well, what with paying for Woojin and Lynx's honeymoon and all…" Clive began.

"Stop it," Blythe cut him off. "I don't know what's gotten into him lately, but he likes pretending that we aren't rich. I think he's trying to set everybody up for a card game or something."

"Have you heard from Wooj?" Joe asked. "They left right after the wedding and we started on vacation the next day."

"They already submitted a report about the independent human communities on Chianga, a Dollnick open world," Clive replied. "Sounded like the humans have gone native and Woojin went native with them. Lynx said something about getting a divorce if he tries eating any faux-Dollnick delicacies in front of her again, but you know how newlyweds are."

"And how's Thomas doing with the training camp?" Joe followed up. "The new group of recruits must have started a few days ago. I've sort of lost track."

"That's what you're supposed to do on vacation," Blythe said over her shoulder, as she rooted around in a dense patch of vines growing on an elaborate arbor. "Just where Libby said they'd be. Give me a hand with these."

Blythe removed a tubular bag from the hidden space, handed it to Kelly, and then rapidly extracted seven more. Kelly passed each bag on to Joe, who tossed them to Clive. The last bag was much heavier, and Blythe's head and upper body vanished into the vines as she wrestled it out.

"What is all this stuff?" Kelly asked.

"Furniture," Blythe explained. "This one is the table."

When the smaller bags were opened, the carbon fiber and fabric chairs practically unfolded themselves on being extracted. The table was another story, but with one adult pulling on each corner, it finally snapped into shape, providing a taut fabric surface that barely budged when Samuel climbed onto it and started jumping.

"Samuel McAllister!" Kelly said in dismay. "That's our dinner table you're jumping on."

"I thought it was a trampoline," he replied innocently.

"Off," Joe said, grabbing his son mid-bounce and putting him down on the deck. "Remember to ask Libby where she dug this stuff up," he added in an aside to his wife. "I might buy a set for the Nova, in case we ever get to go anywhere again."

85

"Hi Aunty Blythe, Uncle Clive," Dorothy called as she approached with Mist. Beowulf conscientiously herded the girls forward, his eyes on the pretzel bag. "Did you meet any of the ghosts?"

"How would I know if I did?" Blythe asked. "I thought they were invisible."

"Not these ghosts," Dorothy said. "And they can talk and talk, but in the end they don't say anything."

"They think a lot of themselves," Mist added.

"As long as they don't eat, they're fine by me," Clive said. He began unpacking food from the insulated chest and setting it on the table. "I hope these pastry things are the same as the ones at Lynx's wedding."

"That would make them nine days old," Blythe cautioned him. "You know Ian hates to throw away food."

"Can I have Thomas do the ceremony when I get married?" Dorothy asked.

"You'll have to ask him," Kelly replied. "Lynx said he even rented an ecumenical personality upgrade from QuickU to get into the spirit of the thing."

After dinner, the children started a game of hide-and-seek, and adults shared a couple of bottles of wine.

"Can you really believe you're starting your second week on vacation?" Blythe asked Kelly. "When's the last time you even talked to Libby?"

"Eight days ago," Kelly said mournfully. "She told me that to get the full benefit of the vacation I shouldn't talk to her or ask anybody about EarthCent. I guess it's working because I haven't really thought about the embassy in days. There's nothing I need to know about, right?"

Clive and Blythe exchanged a private glance. "Right," they both said at the same time.

Eight

"So you're volunteering to help overthrow the Stryx hegemony?" Walter looked Jeeves up and down. "Could I ask what kind of AI you are, exactly?"

"Well, Stryx," Jeeves admitted. "But don't let that and the robot-body fool you. I'm more human than most humans I've met."

"And you believe that humans have the right to free and democratic elections for the purpose of establishing our own government?"

"Absolutely. I've always felt that my elders put too much emphasis on knowledge and experience and not enough on personality," Jeeves asserted. "A million years here, a million years there, that's the Stryx way of looking at things. We're almost as bad as the Makers."

"It seems highly irregular," the HEEL organizer muttered, almost to himself. He paused to look around at the other members of his ad hoc democracy committee who were gathered around Kelly's display desk in the EarthCent embassy. "I don't have any personal objections, of course, but I want to make sure the rest of you are comfortable with—are you sure he's not here to spy on us?"

"I wouldn't have invited Jeeves if I didn't trust him implicitly," Shaina said. "We've been business partners for years, and he went to school with Paul, the ambassador's foster son. Besides, who do you think he's going to spy on us for? The Hortens? The Vergallians?"

"Well, the Stryx," Walter said in exasperation. "Don't they make a lot of money by keeping humanity on a short leash?"

Everybody in the room except for the HEEL organizer burst out in laughter.

"Libby," Daniel said. "Can you show us a balance sheet for the Stryx dealings with humanity?"

"Of course," the librarian replied over the office speakers, causing Walter to twist in his seat and look around wildly. An array of colored spheres appeared floating over the display desk, each revolving slowly to display its label. "The sizes of the spheres show the relative amounts of the subsidies involved versus true market rates. The label on the little white sphere may be too small for you to read, but that's the budget for all of EarthCent's diplomatic operations."

"What's the military assistance item?" Clive asked, leaning forward in his seat to study the data.

"It's an implied expense," Libby replied. "It's the money humans are saving every cycle by not maintaining a military while Earth is under our protection. Jeeves said I shouldn't include it since you never asked for our help, but Gryph overruled him."

"See?" Jeeves said, to nobody in particular.

"How about the second biggest one, the tunnel freight subsidy?" Walter asked. Although he was still in a bit of shock at the sudden intrusion of a number of Stryx advisors to his meeting, you don't make it through a doctoral program at one of Earth's most renowned schools without learning how to cope with verbal sneak attacks. "I heard that the Stryx assess a special tithe on all Earth exports while the other species only pay fixed fees."

"Earth wouldn't have an export industry without the Stryx tunnel subsidies," Shaina explained. "The value of Earth goods isn't enough to pay the standard fees the Stryx charge the other species. And that doesn't even take into account the relatively low capacity and poor efficiency of the ships humans are able to acquire, mainly through Stryx-subsidized loans. Instead of charging for mass and volume, the Stryx take a percentage of the profit. Earth is actually the only planet in the galaxy that can afford to export certain bulky, low-value products, like tissues and toilet paper."

"So what do all the aliens do without toilet paper?" Walter couldn't help asking.

"He's never even been in an all-species bathroom," Shaina said, her face breaking into a wide grin. "Don't you spoil it for him, Daniel," she added, seeing that the helpful junior consul was about to explain.

"So in round figures, how much do all of these subsidies come to?" Walter asked, trying to show that he wasn't embarrassed by his lack of travel experience. "How big of a bill will the Stryx be presenting when we go out on our own?"

"This isn't a bill or even a running tab," Libby replied patiently. "Daniel asked for a balance sheet, and currently, humanity is in the red. The numbers would be a little larger if not for the profit some Stryx earn in business relationships with humans, like my own participation in InstaSitter. When humanity progresses to the point that the subsidies are no longer required, they'll be phased out."

"Forgive me if I seem a little skeptical, but I attended an international academic conference on human exploitation by aliens just last year, and none of this came up in the papers presented," Walter said. "Are you suggesting that even if we vote to close EarthCent and establish our own galactic government, you won't seek repayment?"

"Hang on a second, Walter," Daniel objected. "I don't want to sound like an apparatchik, but I don't see why you're in a hurry to close EarthCent. Humanity doesn't pay our salaries, we don't tell anybody what to do, and we're not a barrier to humans developing self-government."

"But everybody thinks of you as the government," Walter protested.

"Everybody who?" Clive replied, struggling to hold back his laughter. "The aliens all think that EarthCent is some sort of glorified tourist agency for Earth, and most humans have probably never heard of us, much less seen an EarthCent employee. The only place anybody could possibly mistake EarthCent for a government is on the Stryx stations, and that's only because the ambassadors sponsor events and dip into petty cash to give hand-outs to stranded human travelers."

"Listen," Daniel said. "I'm sorry that none of the others from the last meeting showed up, but people on the station are pretty busy. EarthCent Intelligence has sent a couple agents on a fact-finding mission to the human communities starting local governments, and we'll be happy to share that information with you when they return. Personally, I'm fascinated by the concept of elections and I'm willing to help, but I need to believe that there's a point to the whole thing."

"I'm interested even if there isn't a point," Jeeves said.

"Let me show you the materials I received," Walter offered, abandoning the idea that he could simply talk his small audience around to his point of view. He reached into the large duffle bag made of a tough rug-like material that he'd deposited in front of his seat and began to rummage around. "It's not all that original, that's the way it is with universal truths," he added apologetically, pulling out a large coffee mug and placing it on Kelly's display desk.

"No taxation without representation," Daniel read aloud. "What taxation?"

"Well, I guess the tunnel tithes," Walter replied, looking embarrassed.

"After Libby explained that the Stryx lose money on human tunnel traffic and that they pay for EarthCent as well?" Shaina objected. "Humanity has no taxation and free representation under the current deal."

"But that was my favorite," Walter said, looking at the mug sadly. He started rooting through his carpetbag again and pulled out another mug, this one printed with, "One man, one vote."

"I don't get a vote?" Shaina inquired in an icy tone.

"What about human-identifying sentients?" Jeeves inquired.

"They mean 'man' in the universal sense, for humankind, I think," Walter replied. "I did hear back from headquarters on the artificial person's question, and the answer was that human-created AI is welcome. I guess I'll have to ask about you now," he added, turning to Jeeves.

"I realize that a lot of humans like hot drinks, and I know I don't have any expertise in organizing elections, but I think you need a way to get people to show up so you can give them the mugs," Clive said. "How large was the shipment?"

"Just samples. These two and a bunch with sort of violent slogans that didn't make any sense to me," Walter admitted. "But I have a budget to get them printed here on the station. You said your family works in the Shuk, Shaina. Do you have any idea how many printed mugs I could get for ten thousand creds?"

"Ten thousand creds?" she repeated in astonishment. "You could get tens of thousands. The Frunge do them for a few hundred millicreds, but I don't know where you're going to store them. What's your overall budget?"

"Two hundred thousand to start," the HEEL organizer said. For the first time, it was Union Station dwellers who appeared shocked. "What? Is that a lot?"

"That's a huge amount of money for the local rep of a political movement that's coming out of nowhere," Clive told him. "Maybe your budget is larger than the other organizers for some reason, but we've already heard that HEEL agents are showing up on all of the stations with a large human presence, on every world with an EarthCent embassy, and on some of the open worlds as well. If your budget is typical, that means there are tens of millions of creds involved."

"What does HEEL hope to accomplish with all that money?" Daniel asked, leaning over the corner of Kelly's display desk to look into Walter's bag of goodies. "Didn't you get any position papers, or holo-cube presentations, or survey data?"

"There's a bunch of numbered cube-things but I didn't know how they worked," Walter replied. "I was going to ask you after the meeting."

"Find number one," Daniel instructed him. "Just throw it at something hard, like the floor or the wall."

"Or me," Jeeves suggested. "Anything for the cause."

Walter identified the first holo-cube in the series, looked at Jeeves, and then threw it against the wall. A hologram featuring a beautiful woman wearing a partial face mask appeared immediately. She looked like she was dressed for a high-society ball.

"Welcome to the Human Expatriates Election League orientation course," she purred in a husky contralto. "These cubes contain everything you'll need to know to establish a grass-roots organization that will bring about the transition from an EarthCent dictatorship to a representative democracy. If you need to reorder any of the segments to show your staff, please specify the number of the cube."

The holographic figure turned and began walking down a long corridor, causing the viewers to feel they were being drawn deeper into the content. Strains of unidentifiable music swelled as the actress or instructor reached a large metal door and pushed a button in its center. The door disappeared and the perspective suddenly changed, showing the woman standing in front of a large crowd in an amphitheatre.

"Nice effect," Shaina commented. "Haven't seen that one before."

"Democracy can be messy," the HEEL instructor said. The crowd in the amphitheatre all began to shout at each other. "And noisy," she continued without raising her voice, yet somehow they still heard her clearly over the vociferous if indistinct arguments. "But the payoff for choosing a representative form of government can be immense."

A bird's-eye view of a beautiful villa on a picture perfect coastline replaced the amphitheatre, and the perspective zoomed in towards a figure in a chaise lounge, a drink with an umbrella in one hand. It was the same woman, still with the mask.

93

"In the next holo-cube, I'll show you how to establish a network of volunteers who answer directly to you. As these volunteers enlist their own downliners, your status in HEEL will grow, and when elections are held, you'll find yourself transformed from an organizer into a representative. So, congratulations for getting in on the ground floor, and I'll see you in the next cube."

"That was weird," Shaina said, as the hologram winked out. "It reminds me of a presentation I saw when I was just a teenager and my sister and I wanted our father to add cosmetic products to Kitchen Kitsch. The company I contacted sent a whole holo-cube course on selling their products, but it turned out to be more about finding other people to sell their products and taking a commission from their sales, and on the sales of their downliners,"

"Did it work?" Daniel asked.

"Who knows? My father wouldn't let us buy the first batch of samples even though we had our own savings. He said if we wanted to sell cosmetics, we should contact a wholesaler, pick some stock, and he'd pay to give it a try. We still have twenty gross of fruit-flavored lip gloss in storage somewhere."

"Both pitches are an example of multi-level marketing techniques that were common on Earth before the Stryx came," Jeeves informed them. "Some of your regulators accused such businesses of being pyramid schemes, but of course, you could say the same about practically all human economic activities at the time. I don't see any records of pyramid schemes being used in elections, but that's probably due to government censorship."

"He made that last part up," Libby informed them over the office speakers. "Why don't you play the next cube and find out?"

94

Walter shook his head and reached back into his carpetbag, muttering to himself as he searched for the second cube. When he pulled it out, he threw it against the wall with appreciably more force than was required.

"Welcome back to the HEEL course in multi-level organizing," the beautiful instructor said.

Jeeves remained silent, but he looked as smug as a robot can look. This time the instructor was shown walking towards them through an outdoor market populated by cartoonish animations of shoppers and vendors.

"What's with the mask?" Daniel asked. "Are they afraid that the evil EarthCent police are going to hunt her down?"

"Just watch how it works as I start to recruit downliners," the instructor continued. "Let's begin with him."

A cartoon version of a man dressed in Victorian formalwear that would have looked at home in a period Sherlock Holmes immersive obligingly stopped for their instructor and waited to be sold on something.

"Good day, sir. Would you like to end taxation without representation?"

"With all of my heart," the man replied.

"And do you believe in one man, one vote?"

"God save the King, I do," came the strange response.

"Then go forth and tell others," the instructor said. "You have but one life to give for your country."

"Give me liberty or give me death!" the gentleman responded, as if they were exchanging code phrases. A white line popped into existence between the instructor and her convert to democracy.

As the humans sat gaping at the hologram, the action sped up by an order of magnitude, and the Victorian organizer buttonholed one shopper after another. The conversations were indecipherable because the audio was compressed into nothing more than brief squeaks, but in every instance the recruiter was apparently successful, and a blue line appeared tying him to each new recruit.

In the meantime, their instructor continued to spread the word, and the white lines showing first level downliners continued to multiply. The speed of the hologram picked up until everything was a blur, and then suddenly, all of the action stopped. In the center of the hologram stood their instructor, a mass of white lines linking her to a circle of her first-level recruits. Each of those individuals was linked by blue to a further group of converts, who were linked by red to yet a larger group, and some of those already had green lines out to another level.

The masked instructor gathered the white lines in her hands and pulled. All of the cartoon figures in the market-place fell to their knees.

"I'm ready for the election," she said cheerfully. "In the next cube, I'll show you how to get your voters to the polls while discouraging other candidates from doing the same." The hologram dissolved.

"I can't..., I'm not..., I don't know what to say," Walter stuttered.

"I found the presentation refreshingly honest, though the animation was quite crude," Jeeves observed.

"Shouldn't you ping Kelly?" Shaina asked. "If HEEL has as many organizers in the field as we think they do, even if only a fraction of them are successful with this multi-level electioneering thing, it will cause EarthCent problems."

"I hate to bother her on her first vacation since she came to Union Station," Clive said. "Besides, the first thing she would do is ask me for more information, so let's hold off until we get some details from our agents and cultural attachés."

"Can I count on you to keep me in the loop, Walter?" Daniel asked. "I'd hate to see some of the human communities setting up their own governments for the first time falling on their knees to a HEEL organizer who's learned how to pull the strings."

"It's all very confusing," Walter said. "Let me sleep on it."

"If you decide to quit, could you put in a good word for me with your boss?" Jeeves asked. "I'm a very effective public speaker."

Nine

Paul leaned back against the partially disassembled Horten lifeboat he'd been fiddling with and pulled the heat tab actuator on his coffee. There were only a few small family traders parked in the camping and maintenance area of Mac's Bones, and other than tool rentals and a request for help adjusting a fiddly Sharf drive later in the day, they weren't making any demands on Paul's time. The lifeboat was salvage and it would probably end up as scrap, but it was close enough to the small parade ground that Paul could eavesdrop on Thomas addressing the class of recruits without being obvious about it.

"I know that some of you have friends who already work for EarthCent Intelligence and they've probably told you about the training camp," Thomas was saying. "That's why we spent the first week running around the hold, doing jumping jacks and lunging at each other with rubber knives. Physical training and team building exercises are indeed important, but some of us feel that in the short time we have you, more emphasis should be given to the unique skills required by agents in the field."

The line of recruits began to nudge each other and grin. EarthCent Intelligence attracted lots of middle-aged and bookish candidates, and while self-defense demonstrations were fun to watch, getting thrown to the floor by a fellow beginner was always risky. The highlight of training camp so far had been the artificial person's demonstration of tossing playing cards into the air and then spearing them with thrown pencils, but that wasn't the sort of skill you could hope to master in just a few weeks.

"Starting today, I'll be assisted by Chance, our most experienced field agent. She should be here any minute, but she's not exactly a morning artificial person."

A thirty-something woman wearing a handkerchief tied over her straw-blond hair raised a hand.

"Yes, Gretchen," Thomas said. "You don't have to raise your hand."

"What percentage of EarthCent agents are artificial people, sir?"

"I'm glad you asked that question. The total number of EarthCent agents is proprietary business information, so I can't share the percentage until you complete training and officially join the firm. However, I don't see the harm in telling you that Chance and I are the only artificial people currently working for EarthCent Intelligence."

"What special skills will you teach us?" inquired a middle-age man, who as a recreational jogger, was somewhat disappointed to hear that physical training would be deemphasized. He had enjoyed leaving the younger men behind.

"Let me ask you something," Thomas said in reply. "What skills do you think are vital for agents in the field?"

"Running?" the jogger suggested.

"Surveillance?" Gretchen offered.

"Spearing playing cards with pencils?" a young man said hopefully.

"Assassination techniques?"

Everybody turned to look at the fierce young woman who had cut the sleeves off of her T-shirt on the first day of training camp. Blythe warned Thomas that Judith had badly failed the InstaSitter personality test that was also used as a screen for EarthCent Intelligence recruits, although the cut-off score was set much lower for spies. But now that all of the cultural attaché and information analyst positions were well-staffed, Clive insisted they loosen the standard even further to start accepting more aggressive candidates.

"Dancing," Chance declared, breaking the silence and suppressing a yawn as she sauntered up to the group. "Sorry I'm late, but, no, I don't really have an excuse."

"Dancing it is," Thomas said, ignoring the latter part of Chance's statement. "We can't compete with the advanced species in surveillance technology, especially since we're using their own equipment. And while throwing pencils, running and assassination are all useful skills, they share in common the trait that they're only needed if all else fails. I hope we aren't training you for failure here. The primary mission of EarthCent Intelligence agents in the field is to gather information, both personally and through building networks of sources. And how do you think this is done?"

"Money?" the jogger suggested.

"Artificial intelligence," Gretchen said.

"Blackmail?" Judith guessed.

"Socializing," Chance said. "How are you going to sound out a prospect or ask questions if you don't get them into a conversation?"

Still leaning against the lifeboat, Paul had given up any attempt to pretend that he was busy working. Since Chance had stopped by the previous night to ask for his help in setting up for a new training exercise, he'd been trying to figure out how she was going to lead into it.

Somehow he doubted that the artificial people had run the idea past Joe and Woojin.

"But none of us are as beautiful as you, as either of you," protested an attractive young woman with apparent self-esteem issues.

"What's your name?" Chance asked.

"Bonnie-Sue."

"That's a great name," Chance said. "If my name was Bonnie-Sue, I bet I could sign up twice as many informants."

"You're just saying that to make me feel better," Bonnie-Sue protested, though she couldn't stop herself from blushing.

"No, I'm saying it to show you how to pick up guys in bars," Chance explained. "I'm always seeing sentients let the opportunity to connect with somebody slip by because they think you need to come up with the perfect line. Now I just gave you two."

"Try them on me now," Thomas suggested to Bonnie-Sue.

"Uh, hi. What's your name?"

"I'm Thomas."

"You're really good-looking, Thomas," Bonnie-Sue said, and then she turned bright red in embarrassment. "Wait, I messed that up. What was it I was supposed to say? Uh, can I buy you a drink?"

"You're going too fast," Chance told her. "When sentients give you their names, they've basically authorized you to start a conversation on the subject. I've been making a study of techniques for getting acquainted with strangers, and if you can get two responses out of the average target, you've gained their trust enough to start complaining about work or travel. Now watch us."

Chance took a few steps in the direction of Paul, then turned around and walked towards Thomas as if she was seeing him for the first time.

"Hi. What's your name?" she asked, offering him friendly smile number four from her catalog.

"I'm Thomas," he replied, looking a bit wary.

"Thomas. That's a great name. My little brother is a Thomas."

"You have a little brother?" Thomas asked. "How come you never told me?"

Chance made a circle by placing the tip of her middle finger behind the last joint on her thumb and then flicked Thomas on the forehead.

"Ouch!" he exclaimed, rubbing the spot. "What was that?"

"That was me showing the ladies how to deal with a wise-guy in a bar," Chance told him. She turned back to the recruits. "Did everybody get that? Good. Before we pair up to practice meeting strangers, I need to make sure you're all familiar with role-playing. Do you know what I mean by role-playing?"

"Acting?" the jogger guessed.

"What's your name?" Chance asked him.

"Stephen."

"Huh," Chance grunted. Stephen's face fell when his name failed to meet with the artificial person's approval.

"You're role-playing somebody. Right?" Gretchen asked.

"Exactly," Chance replied with a dazzling smile. "That was me playing the part of the typical guy who asks my name and then gets tongue-tied. Now I'll play the role of a deep space trader who has just returned to a Stryx station and has been drinking in a bar, and you try getting some

102

useful information from me. Pretend we've already covered the names subject and we've both had a few drinks. No, wait a sec," she said, fumbling around in her pocketbook for a tube of her favorite goth lipstick. She turned her back to them for a moment, and when she turned around again, she sported the steely if somewhat out of focus gaze of a tipsy deep space trader, and a drawn-on mustache.

"So, how about going back to my room, Gretch?" Chance asked in a low tone.

Gretchen giggled and looked around self-consciously at the other trainees. "Uh, sure, I guess."

"No," Chance said, reverting to her usual vocal register. "What do you think his mind is going to be on if you go back to his room? Besides, if you want a man to respect you, never go home with him right away."

"I never would," Gretchen said, blushing again. "I was role-playing."

"Hmm, maybe I led you down the garden path there, but the point of this exercise was to get you to think about what sorts of questions to ask a stranger after you've gotten past the introduction. Anybody?"

"How is your ship armed?" Judith asked.

The artificial person with the mustache shook her head in disapproval. "Too fast."

"Visit any interesting worlds lately?" Stephen tried.

"That's better," Chance said.

"So how should I have answered your invitation?" Gretchen asked.

"Here," Chance said, throwing her the black lipstick. "You be me, I mean, him. Let's take it from the top this time. Alright?"

Gretchen hastily drew an uneven mustache above her lip.

Chance sashayed over to the trainee, took back her lipstick, and said, "Hi. What's your name?"

"Gretchen," the trainee replied, though her voice cracked a little from trying to sound like a man.

"Gretchen. That's a great name. I once had a crush on a guy named Gretchen."

"Want to go back to my place?" Gretchen asked hopefully.

"I just got here," Chance replied, brushing an imaginary speck of dust off of the recruit's sleeve. "It sounds like you've been away from civilization for a while."

"I get it," Bonnie-Sue said excitedly. "If I was her, him, I'd start listing all the places I'd visited."

"Giving him an excuse to talk about spending a long time on the road works on everybody except for a real lady's man," Chance told them. "Now I'm going to hand out some cards from a mercantile board game that Drazen children play, but don't worry, I've written in the translations for each line. They basically provide your identity, starting with your species and ending with the most valuable item in your cargo."

"So it's role-playing," Gretchen said.

"That's right," Thomas reentered the discussion. "It's secret agent role-playing instead of soldier-in-boot-camp role-playing."

"We've got some chairs set up in front of the ice harvester," Chance continued. "We're all going to go over there, pair off, and see how you do extracting information from each other. Everybody has to drink a couple of beers to keep it realistic, but try to stay in your role. And remember, it's not a contest to see who can keep secrets. It's an exercise to practice hearing what somebody is saying and guiding the conversation in the direction you want it to go."

"I don't drink beer in the morning," one of the younger recruits said dubiously.

"Then it's time you learned," Chance replied, ushering them towards the improvised beer garden.

"I don't drink alcohol at all," a middle-aged woman complained.

"Then it's time you learned to fake it," Chance said in exasperation. "Paul has volunteered to play bartender for us, so order a mixed drink without the alcohol and give him a good tip so he doesn't blab. Thomas, help Paul bring up as many pitchers as you can manage, and I'll get the trainees seated and hand out the Drazen cards."

Paul and Thomas strode out ahead of the pack and entered the ice harvester at deck level, utilizing the side port that led directly into Joe's brewing room.

"Did you know that this was what she was planning?" Paul asked.

"I thought we were going to focus on dancing today, but we talked about doing bar interrogations as well."

"Maybe she looked over the recruits and decided they could use a few beers before hitting the dance floor," Paul said. "I know I do."

"I didn't think of that," Thomas replied, looking thoughtful. "How about we just bring out a keg, like you do for picnics?"

"Makes sense to me," Paul concurred. "We'll take the tapped one, but let's try to avoid sloshing or I'll get nothing but foam until it settles down."

It took them a few minutes to move the keg around to the patio area at the front of the ice harvester where the folding tables and chairs were set up. Chance had finished pairing off all of the recruits and was making sure that everybody understood the roles they were to play.

"I need a different card," a large man with the weather-beaten face and hands of an ex-ag world laborer declared.

"Even if it's the exact opposite of who you are, it's important to learn how to adapt," Chance replied patiently.

"It's not that," the man said. "The card says I'm the dominant male in a Fillinduck trio, but I've never even heard of Fillinducks."

"Sorry," Chance said, exchanging cards with him. "Does anybody else have an identity they can't work with?"

"I can manage a Horten I think, but I don't understand what my cargo is," another man complained.

"Let me see your card," Chance said. She glanced down the items, scratched one out, and wrote in a new line. "Here. Does that work for you?"

"Perfect," the would-be Horten replied with a grin.

"Alright. Everybody grab your plastic cup and queue up for a beer," Chance instructed. "I'm going inside to get a bottle of grain alcohol for me and some fruit juice for fake mixed drinks. And remember, there's no such thing as morning in the spy business."

As the unnamed period before lunch wore on, the volume of the conversations taking place steadily increased until some of the trainees were practically shouting. Chance and Thomas each strolled independently among the tables, listening in for a few minutes here, offering a suggestion there, but on the whole, they allowed the recruits to find their own way. After two hours, Thomas and Paul returned the much-lighter keg to the brew room.

"Time's up," Chance announced, clapping her hands loudly to get their attention. "Settle down, settle down. We have a little time before we break for lunch, and I want to get your feedback on this exercise and how you did with it while the impression is still fresh. Does anybody think they figured out the cargo of the person they talked to?"

All of the recruits raised a hand.

"Cool," Chance said. "Did any of you cheat and check if you were right?"

The recruits shook their heads in the negative.

"Great. I want you to exchange cards with the person across from you and see how you did."

Twenty cards were exchanged across the table, and then the groans and laughs began. Chance shushed everybody and picked the closest couple to share their conclusions.

"I thought you were playing a Drazen," exclaimed the man who'd been sitting across from Gretchen. "And you practically told me that your cargo was replacement parts for a Sharf racer."

"Me? A Drazen?"

"You've been playing with your tentacle all day!"

"That's my ponytail," Gretchen protested. "How did you read a tentacle into it? And all that talk about replacement parts for a Sharf racer was your idea. I was just pretending to be interested so you'd keep talking. How come you led me on about your cargo being women's clothing? I was ready to buy a skirt from you."

"You brought up clothes and stopped listening," the man objected. "I told you three times that I don't know a thing about women's clothes and I'm not interested in learning."

"I thought if you were being so vehement about it you must be hiding something," Gretchen admitted.

"Excellent," Chance complimented them. "Now, how many of you had the same experience this morning?"

One hand went up, then two, then four more, and then all of the recruits had their hands raised.

"Does anybody remember Thomas or myself telling you to stop asking the same question different ways and to move on to another subject?"

All of the hands went down, then a few guilty-looking recruits raised them halfway, and then the entire group followed suit.

"So how many of you, after a couple of beers or high-fructose fruit juices, ended up talking about your favorite subjects rather than trying to find out what the other person was interested in?"

There were some embarrassed grins, but all of the hands stayed up.

"That's fine for a first try, in fact, I'm glad it worked out this way," Chance said. "When the job is socializing and having a good time, it's easy to lose track of the fact that it's still a job. But if you want EarthCent Intelligence to pay your bar tabs, you have to produce something other than a shopping list."

"A-B-A," Thomas said, drawing the letters in the air with a finger. "Always Be Asking. There may come a time in your career when you'll be assigned to obtain a particular piece of intelligence, but for now, our idea of a good spy is somebody who goes somewhere and learns everything the natives know. The only way to do that is to ask questions and listen to the answers."

"Alright, let's break for lunch, and we'll take an extra hour today in case you want to squeeze in a nap on the wrestling mats. This afternoon will be dancing with aliens, so ladies, bring your heels if you have them."

Ten

"Come in," a musical voice sang over the speaker in response to Woojin's pushing the door bell. Lynx and Woojin took a moment to brush the snow off of each other's hoods and coats, and stamped their feet on the grating to free the ice from the deep treads in the soles of their survival boots before entering.

"I'm Lynx and he's Woojin," Lynx announced as they entered the warm room. "Thank you for agreeing to see us on such short notice. I apologize in advance that we didn't quite get your name or your official title over the comm because the reception was terrible."

"Joan Powell. I'm the designated stakeholder," replied the delicate woman who met them. She ushered her guests to a pair of low chairs positioned in front of a desk on a raised pedestal, where she took her own seat. "I see you don't recognize my title, but the best human analogy would be akin to my holding a temporary and revocable power-of-attorney for all of the stakeholders in the consortium."

"For the Two Mountains consortium?" Lynx asked in surprise. "I know a young Drazen woman who has an executive position in a human business on Union Station, but I've never heard of a Drazen consortium putting a human in charge."

The woman burst out in tinkling laughter which was so contagious that Woojin joined in. Lynx glared at her husband, which only made him laugh harder.

"Oh, my word," Joan exclaimed, when she finally caught her breath. "The Two Mountains consortium owns this entire planet. Our human consortium can't even afford to pay the Drazens for an enhanced comm link, which is why we had trouble talking earlier. You arrived during the high season for sunspots."

"The Drazens charge that much for a satellite channel?" Woojin asked.

"I should have said that we get so few visitors that it just doesn't make economic sense to pay the subscription fee," Joan corrected herself. "I have to answer to the stakeholders for expenses, and none of the women would be very happy with me if there was no money for phinter strings because I spent it on a luxury like spread spectrum communications."

"What do you do with phinter strings?" Lynx asked. "I remember a trader telling me that they only come from the tails of the Drazen equivalent of a unicorn and they're worth a thousand times their weight in gold."

"We use them to restring our phinters, of course," Joan replied, seemingly puzzled by the question. "The only other application I know of is for strangling a regicide, but that may only be in fables."

"Drazen fables?" Woojin inquired.

"Certainly," Joan said. "It would be strange if phinter strings appeared in human fables when we had no knowledge they even existed. But I'm sure you didn't come all the way from Union Station to talk to me about our amateur musical efforts. I believe you said something about EarthCent in your initial transmission?"

110

"That's right," Lynx replied. "We're both employed by EarthCent Intelligence, and it recently came to our attention that self-governing human communities are taking hold on some of the alien worlds where they're permitted. We've been tasked to open a dialogue with the new governments and offer whatever assistance we can, other than financial, of course."

"Of course," Joan echoed with a smile. "Would your timing have anything to do with the recent arrival of a regional organizer from the Human Expatriates Election League?"

"We just got married a few weeks ago," Lynx replied. "Our boss offered us this assignment as a working honeymoon."

"Good business," the designated stakeholder said, nodding her head in approval. "Well, you just missed the HEEL organizer in any case. I'm afraid that some of our more active stakeholders ran him off the planet. I tried to explain to them that he wasn't attempting to stage a hostile takeover, but I'm afraid that's how they interpreted all of his talk about combining shares to elect board members. Somebody cued him into our bylaws at the last minute, and he requested that I issue him a temporary LLO statement authorizing him to stay, but frankly, he didn't have a tentacle to hang from."

"An LLO?" Woojin asked.

"Licensed Labor Organizer," Joan elucidated. "If he had requested an LLA, Licensed Labor Agitator, I might have given it to him, for the entertainment value if nothing else. He really didn't seem to have the foggiest notion of how we live here, but he was well-funded, and it's not hard to get an audience in a bar if you're willing to pay for the Divverflips."

"That bubbling drink the macho Drazen guys pour down?" Lynx asked in disbelief "The one traders use to clean space lichen off of their hulls? I bought a Divverflip once to try cleaning up some stains in my hold, but it ate through the thermos before I got back to my ship."

The designated stakeholder burst out laughing a second time, reaching back and gripping her ponytail with one hand, as if it were a tentacle that could pop up and embarrass her.

"They aren't entirely authentic," Joan said. "Our bartenders cut way back on the concentration of some of the acids, they just leave enough to make your lips tingle. My husband and son drink them, but males will be males. That's why we don't give them any say in how to run the household."

"We really don't know anything about your situation here," Woojin said. "The Drazen ambassador on Union Station told us that it's a recent development for a consortium to grant even limited autonomy to so large a settlement of aliens living on a productive world, but you seem to be ahead of the curve."

"Not many Drazen colonists wanted to live this far north due to the cold, but changing the axial tilt of the planet for a larger temperate zone is expensive," Joan explained. "Two Mountains granted us a sub-charter as an independent consortium with mineral rights above the sixtieth parallel, subject to their receiving a fifty-percent cut and four seats on the board. All of us either worked for Two Mountains or grew up in their company towns, and we regard the sub-charter as a production bonus for completing the two-generation labor contract that brought our families to this planet in the first place."

The designated stakeholder halted her exposition and sniffed the air with an intent look on her face. She rose from her chair, sniffing as she went, and worked her way around to where Lynx and Woojin were seated. Lynx managed an embarrassed smile as the woman sniffed around the collar of her coat before giving Woojin the same treatment.

"Have you been eating Blue Snakees?" Joan asked him.

"Spoon worms, imported from Korea and farmed on Chianga."

"Chianga! That's why I thought they were Blue Snakees. We trade with the humans there because they make great floaters and serviceable power packs, but they keep sending me these faux-Dollnick delicacies on every Prince's Day."

"So you're not big fans of Dollnick fare," Woojin hazarded a guess.

"Most of it is poisonous and the rest tastes like tentacle mange," she replied dismissively. "I'd be the last person to suggest that humans ignore the cultivated tastes of the superior cultures we've come in contact with, but Dollnicks?"

"I'm with you a hundred percent, as long as I don't have to drink a Divverflip," Lynx volunteered.

"You know, we've been talking with the Chiangans about getting together on neutral ground sometime. We want to look for areas of cooperation that would allow us to cut overhead costs," Joan said. "We trade with several other independent human communities on Dollnick and Verlock worlds, but somehow we never manage to get together in the same place to discuss the broader issues. I suppose it's because none of us are prepared to acknowledge another one of our group as the leader."

113

"Use us," Lynx offered immediately. "Our embassy on Union Station is always hosting conferences and trade shows. Our ambassador and the local Stryx are highly supportive of inter-species cooperation. It's like their main thing."

"Are you suggesting that the stakeholders in our consortium are a different species than the humans on Chianga or Union Station?" Joan asked, with a twinkle in her eye.

"I've been married to her for three weeks, and we've known each other for years, but she still thinks I'm from a different species," Woojin said to cover Lynx's slip.

"You are," his wife muttered under her breath.

"Do you have any idea how much something like a conference/trade show package would cost?" Joan asked. "I could justify bringing along some team leaders and mineral samples if there was a commercial component, but I imagine that food and lodging on a Stryx station can add up. The tunnel charges alone are probably more than we can manage."

"I wouldn't be at all surprised if EarthCent Intelligence would foot the bill for the whole thing," Woojin said. "While I primarily work in training and contingency planning, I know that the agency runs at a profit by trading on business intelligence, and I suspect our money people will figure out how to make a profit on you as well."

The designated stakeholder broke into a wide smile. "You couldn't have brought better news. I was worried that you came to lecture us about the joys of representative government run by professional parasites, like that HEEL man. What a relief to hear that EarthCent has its business priorities straight. Can I take the two of you on a tour of our mines?"

"No worms or Divverflips?" Lynx asked.

"Just a few hundred thousand hard-working stakeholders tunneling under mountains," Joan replied. "I have a Chiangan floater out back, so we can be at the closest entrance and out of the weather in five minutes."

As the floater zipped its three occupants across the frozen tundra to the sound of a women's choral group coming over the hidden speakers, Woojin and Lynx wondered at the strange layout of the town.

"I was so happy to see your office and get out of the snow that it didn't occur to me to ask why you're stuck out at the landing field," Woojin finally said. "It seems like a pretty noisy location for the effective manager of a consortium."

"As designated stakeholder, I have a fiscal responsibility to see that all of our product is fairly weighed and credited," Joan replied. "I know that in Earth corporations that would be a low-level job, but we hold by the Drazen approach that you have no place at the top if you don't know the bottom inside-out."

"Oh, I think I heard a saying about that from a Drazen friend," Lynx commented.

"Be the job," Joan quoted.

"No, it had something to do with leadership."

"For clean management, follow the janitor," Joan suggested.

"That's a good one too, but I think the ambassador was referring to his work in the immersives, if that helps."

"If you have to act like you know what you're doing, start again at the bottom."

115

"That's it," Lynx said. "Bork told me that one when I mentioned the difficulties I was having representing EarthCent at some of the sporting events our ambassador skipped. I'm also the cultural attaché for the Union Station embassy, but I can't keep up with some of these alien sports, including Drazen Crackback."

"You can ask my husband later, he and my son play in the local league. All of the men do."

"But you need a tentacle," Lynx protested.

"They use prosthetics. Here we are, now duck your heads because I'm going to drop the fields and it's a low entry."

The cold wind briefly returned as the floater stopped right before the entry to the mine. A sensor detected their presence, retracted the door, and the floater crept in, the gunwales barely clearing the roof.

"Just keep your heads down," the driver warned her guests. "There's a parking area up on the right here, and then we'll change to a rail car."

"Floaters don't hold up in the mines?" Woojin guessed.

"The filters keep clogging, but the main problem is weight capacity," Joan said, as she eased the floater into the crudely hewn chamber, holding her head sideways as she peered over the dashboard. When she set it down, there was just enough room to climb out and move back to the main passage in a crouch. "The energy balance just doesn't make sense when you're transporting tons of ore out of a mine. We'd end up spending more on energy packs than the Yttrium yield can justify."

"Is that your main product here?"

"Oh, we make use of everything one way or another. You won't find any tailing piles outside of Drazen mines," the human said proudly. "Most of the metal ores are smelted for local construction and manufacturing materials. Even with the space elevators in the South, it's tough to compete with the asteroid mining outfits that work the inner belts of this system. But the Yttrium is all for export, and most of it goes back to the Drazen home world for high-temperature superconductors that they use in military applications, like rail guns."

Still crouching, the three humans clambered into a heavily built rail car with permanently reclining seats that lowered the required ceiling clearance. The touch panel that controlled the car was the only part that didn't look like somebody had pounded on it with a sledge hammer for a few decades. There were glow lamps strung all along the main passage, and five rails, spaced oddly, ran along the floor on metal ties.

"What's the point of the fifth rail?" Woojin asked, as the mining car began to move forward with a lurch.

"It's a monorail for emergency worker evacuation," Joan explained. "The Two Mountains consortium has never treated its human workers as expendable, so when it comes to our husbands and sons, we could hardly do less."

"Is that singing I hear coming from hidden speakers?" Lynx asked over the noise produced by their transportation.

"Just wait a bit and you'll see," Joan responded, as the car rumbled down the tracks.

A minute later, the mining car emerged from the tunnel into an enormous cavern, which was lit from the ceiling by bright floodlights. The rails grew sidings in the subterranean switchyard, spreading out like the branches of a river delta where it meets the sea. Thousands of men in dirty coveralls were at work with pneumatic tools and alien-looking scanning devices, sorting raw ore from piles, breaking up larger chunks, and distributing the minerals into marked carriers. The walls of the cavern were penetrated by dozens of tunnels heading further under the mountains, each with its own set of tracks, plus the extra monorail.

"There you have your answer," Joan said, bringing their car to a halt on a siding. A choir of at least a hundred women, all dressed in formal black robes, were belting out a remarkably complex vocal arrangement. "Turn off your implant if you're using one," their guide urged Lynx and Woojin. "Simultaneous translation doesn't do justice to choral music, especially the more advanced Drazen compositions."

To describe the beauty of the singing as unearthly would be redundant, since the performance was taking place hundreds of light years from Earth and the composer was a member of an alien race. But even without the translation, the EarthCent agents felt invigorated by the music, which produced an overwhelming sense of contributing positively to civilization. Woojin even started forward, looking for some task he could do to aid in the community effort, but the designated stakeholder reached out and took hold of his arm.

"You'd just be in the way," she told him. "Don't feel bad. The music has that effect on everybody with a heart."

"So the women sing and the men do all the work," Lynx said, after she recovered from her initial wave of emotion.

"Most of the women in our community come and sing for an hour each day. The men have a system for swapping jobs between mining and working in the sorting hall which makes little sense to us, but nothing men do makes much sense, does it?" she added, nudging Lynx. "We take our singing very seriously, and truth be told, the main reason I got this job was for my solo performances."

"You have singing contests instead of elections?"

"It's more like popular acclamation," Joan said, looking a bit embarrassed. "One day, after I sang, 'Beat Your Drills and Shovels into Axe Blades,' the miners all stopped working and declared they wouldn't start again until I was appointed the new designated stakeholder. I found out afterwards that Livia, my predecessor, had asked them to select somebody that week because the job was wearing on her."

"Do you have Drazens working here?" Woojin asked suddenly.

"For what we can afford to pay?" Joan replied incredulously. "Why do you ask?"

Woojin indicated with his head a group of men who were running scanners over a carload of ore that had just arrived through one of the small tunnels. "I kept my optical amplification implant after I retired from the mercenaries, and all of the men working in that group have six fingers."

Joan fished around in her belt pouch and brought out the strangest looking pair of gloves the visitors had ever seen. All of the fingers were cut off except for the thumb on one side. The designated stakeholder pulled on the gloves and demonstrated the grip of her prosthetic second thumbs by shaking hands with Woojin and Lynx in turn.

"I think I mentioned that our men practice with prosthetic tentacles in order to play sports, but the gloves are essential to operate some Drazen equipment and musical instruments. We're about the same size as the Drazens otherwise, and we don't have the industrial base to redesign all of their tools for human use, like the Chiangans do

119

with Dollnick technology," she explained. "And really, the extra thumb comes in handy. Sometimes I put the gloves on and forget to take them off all day."

"Would it be possible for us to meet with any of the other community leaders?" Woojin asked. "And even though you already resolved the issue, I'd like to hear more about the HEEL organizer's visit, if possible."

"We have a grand choral practice tonight. I can request that the section leaders stay after as long as you're willing to pay for refreshments."

"As long as you can accept a programmable cred," Woojin responded. "It's on our EarthCent Intelligence expense account that way."

"There's a register in the symphony hall café," Joan replied. "You're lucky, because there's not another register in the human settlements. Our shops all work off the consortium credit lists or Drazen currency."

"If the chorus is all women, does that mean the men don't take part in the community leadership?" Lynx asked.

"Men grab most of the official management positions, but women take care of the family finances, and that extends to the consortium, which is like a family," Joan replied. "I may be biased after growing up in a Two Mountains mining town, but humans everywhere could do worse than imitating the Drazens."

Eleven

"It reminds me of Mac's Bones when I first took over," Joe declared, staring out over the towering piles of junk.

"I'm not ready to camp out in a dump," Kelly objected. "I'm still trying to figure out how to explain to our friends that we spent our first week of vacation in a sewer plant and the second week on a ghost deck."

"Who are you going to have to explain to?" Joe replied. "They've all come out to see us."

"And they were all hiding something from me," Kelly said, changing the subject. "I can feel it in my bones. Either the broadcast of my interview with Srythlan triggered a war with the Verlocks, or Daniel has sold the embassy to the Dollnicks and blown the proceeds in a casino."

"You know that Libby asked them all not to talk about work. Even Bork and Czeros went along with it." Joe paused and broke out laughing. "I'd give my left arm for a holo-recording of Czeros bawling out those ghosts. I guess living with his not-quite-deceased ancestors has used up his store of patience for talking with the gone but not departed."

"Can we look around now?" Samuel asked impatiently. "I promised Ailia to find her a queen's treasure to replace the one she lost."

"Good luck with that in here," Joe said skeptically, running his professional eye over the mountains of scrap.

121

"Don't climb on the heaps or try to pull anything out at the bottom because the whole thing could collapse on you. Stand back and ask Banger to do it—he's indestructible. And if you find a passage to the other side, come back and tell us," he added, as the children ran off.

"You've really come to trust Banger, haven't you?" Kelly commented. "I don't remember you letting Dorothy run off with Metoo at that age."

"Metoo was the first six-year-old Stryx I knew and I didn't trust Dorothy's influence over him," Joe replied, glancing after the girls, who had set out with Beowulf on their own accord. "Banger seems a lot more in control somehow."

"So why do you think Libby brought us to a giant junkyard?"

"Nostalgia?" Joe suggested.

"No, there's a method to her madness, something we haven't worked out yet," Kelly insisted, looking around as if she expected to spot a telltale clue. "I hope there's an open field at the campsites, something with nature, no matter how alien. I'd hate to spend the whole week with nothing but abandoned recycling for scenery."

"Then it's amazing that you married me. Although now that I think about it, you didn't see Mac's Bones until after we tied the knot. Besides, maybe all of this stuff was nature for somebody. If your species was made out of metals and plastics, this might feel like a visit to the countryside."

"Ugh, I just had a thought," Kelly said, coming to a halt and shivering against her will. "What if all this scrap is them? Maybe this whole deck is a giant graveyard."

"Naw," Joe replied, peering at one of the piles. "It's old, but a lot of it is bits and pieces of decommissioned ships and equipment. I even recognize some of the parts because the alien manufacturers don't change proven designs until something really better comes along."

"Is that a robot arm?" Kelly said, coming up and taking her husband's elbow as she pointed.

"Eight fingers," Joe observed. "Either they didn't make them in their own likeness, or it's a species we never came across. Maybe I'll call back Banger and ask him."

"Don't bother. He'll only say that Libby would prefer he doesn't tell us. I'm beginning to wonder if we're the only family in the galaxy on a vacation arranged by an omniscient librarian who refuses to answer questions. Hey, it looks like the kids have found something."

"Over here, Daddy! I think the pile moved," Dorothy called in an excited voice. Joe and Kelly jogged over to where Mist and Dorothy were standing very close together. Beowulf pawed tentatively at the edges of a large pile of odd robotic skeletons.

"What is it, boy?" Joe asked the dog. Beowulf turned and shook his giant head, obviously puzzled. It was a familiar scent, but differentiating between metal alloys by smell in the middle of a scrap yard was beyond even the Huravian hound's ability.

"I told you it's a graveyard," Kelly said mournfully. "All we need now are AI ghosts."

The whole heap of scrap suddenly shifted a few inches and everybody jumped.

"Banger! Keep the kids at a safe distance," Joe called, pulling Mist and Dorothy away from the pile. Beowulf continued sniffing at the edges, jerking away at the slightest movement, only to return.

The side of the pile began to bulge out as randomly interlocked pieces of scrap shifted, and in some cases fell away to clatter on the deck. Joe continued to hold back the family, but Beowulf remained undaunted. He even dashed in and pulled off a piece with a massive paw in an attempt to unearth whatever it was quicker.

Slowly, like a mythical swamp creature emerging from the shallows all covered with plants and vines, a large robotic form forced its way out of the pile. It shed smaller bits of junk like water, and picked off the larger pieces and cables with its hands.

Dorothy and Mist pointed and shrieked, but Beowulf just cocked his head, and Banger came up and hovered over him. When the large robot, bigger than an alpha-Dollnick, finally stood clear of the pile, its chest began to crack open. The girls screamed again, this time with Samuel and Ailia joining in.

"Metoo!" Dorothy exclaimed, as her Stryx friend floated out of the cavity in the robot's chest. "What are you doing in there?"

"Jeeves tricked me," the teenage Stryx replied. "Farth finally said I was caught up enough on my multiverse studies to come visit you on vacation, and Jeeves invited himself along. He said you'd all be pleased if I could demonstrate how one of these old exoskeleton units work, but once I got inside, he pushed a whole mound of scrap on top of me and told me to count to infinity or he'd turn the whole mess into atom soup. Do you know how hard it is to get atom soup off your casing?"

"How long ago was that?" Joe asked, looking around cautiously. He wouldn't put it past Jeeves to be hiding somewhere, waiting to push a stack of scrap onto Banger.

"Twenty minutes and eighteen seconds, give or take some smaller units," Metoo replied. "That's how long it usually takes me to count to infinity. How long does it take you?"

"We can't count to infinity, silly," Dorothy retorted, regaining her composure. "It's not possible."

"Sure it is," Metoo replied. "You just have to go so fast that you start gaining on it, and before you know it, infinity gets left behind. It wouldn't be possible to create singularities otherwise."

"It's great to see you, Metoo," Kelly said, hoping to cut the math lesson off as quickly as possible. The young Stryx was always happy to explain things to his human friends, but Kelly had long since learned that the explanations made her head ache while leaving her none the wiser. "Is Jeeves still around, or did he run away?"

"Who questions the great and powerful Jeeves?" boomed a bass voice, followed by the loud clank-clank of robotic steps on a metallic deck. Another ambulatory exoskeleton marched into view from between two mounds of scrap, this one dragging a whole line of exoskeletons behind it on a cable, like a string of freshly caught fish. The last of the tethered mechanical nightmares had four limbs and a tail.

"Does Libby know you're here?" Kelly asked suspiciously. She fought the urge to subvoc her librarian friend.

"She asked me to come and help," the mischievous Stryx replied. "I already told Paul about it, and he'll be coming by later to try one on."

"Try on? You mean you expect us to get inside those things?" Kelly asked.

"Cool," Samuel said. "Can I have the big one?"

"Are you going to explain what they are, Metoo?" Dorothy asked, catching her brother as he dashed forward.

"I guess it's alright since the owners aren't left to explain and Libby isn't telling me to stop," Metoo replied. "The biologicals who lived in these things have been gone a long time, but Libby asked Jeeves to put a bunch of exoskeletons back into working order."

"What happened to the previous owners?" Kelly asked. "Did they move on to better technology, or figure out how to free their minds from their bodies like the ghosts?"

"No, they just sort of atrophied, and eventually they stopped having children," Metoo explained. "Libby made Jeeves take all the life support stuff out of the exoskeletons, since they used to directly inject nutrition, handle waste and all of the vital functions. They even developed exoskeletons that could be expanded over time, so you could start a baby in a little one."

"Gross!" Mist said. "Who would do that to a baby?"

"The biologicals who created the exoskeletons," Metoo replied, taking the question literally.

"Would it make me strong so I could get revenge for my family?" Ailia asked.

Everybody fell silent for a moment. Then Jeeves said, "Step right up, young lady, and you'll find out. Everything is one hundred percent safe and approved for audiences of all ages. I even washed them out."

Samuel ran forward towards the biggest exoskeleton, but Jeeves intercepted him. "They're sized for the humanoid," the Stryx told him. "You'll control them by moving your limbs like normal, but it won't work if your arms and legs aren't long enough to reach the joints."

"Let me go first so they see how it works," Joe said, walking over to the largest exoskeleton, which Samuel was reluctant to abandon. "You just dragged them around on the floor like that? Are you sure they aren't damaged?"

"The mechanisms are practically indestructible, as you can see," Jeeves said, reaching down and triggering the chest cavity of the large exoskeleton to open. "Think of them as suits, like suits of armor, but with power assist and a few other enhancements."

Joe let his backpack slide to the floor, and then he half climbed, half squirmed, into the exoskeleton. It reminded him of putting on an armored spacesuit, except the head was already attached. As soon as he was in, Jeeves flipped the chest panels shut and the suit powered up. From lying on his back, Joe rose to his feet without pushing off from the floor with his arms, moving like an expert limbo dancer who had just gone under the pole.

"Wow. I feel like I could wade right through these piles of junk," Joe said. "One of these suits would have been really handy back when we were still in the recycling business."

"I want to try now," Samuel pleaded, tugging on the leg of the suit Jeeves occupied. "Where's my robot suit?"

"Here you go," Jeeves replied, lifting the boy gently and depositing him in a small suit. As soon as the chest panels swung closed, Samuel was off and running.

"This is great!" he said. "Can I wear this to school?"

"The suits have to stay on this deck," Metoo told them. "And don't start punching the bulkheads or the spokes. That's the only thing that might damage them."

Ailia took possession of the other small exoskeleton suit, and then Dorothy and Mist clambered into the mid-sized models. Kelly hung back with Beowulf and Banger, forming a tripartite axis of skepticism.

"Come on, boy," Joe called, unhooking the four legged exoskeleton from the tow line and standing it upright so the giant dog could see it was intended for him. "Don't you want to be able to run fast and jump high?"

Beowulf crouched a little and then leapt into the air, high over their heads. Having misinterpreted the purpose of the exoskeleton Joe was displaying, he wanted to prove that he couldn't be replaced by some alien robot dog, but he overdid the jump. On a planet with gravity it wouldn't have mattered, but on a spinning space station where the only weight came from angular acceleration, jumping so high on a random vector was a miscalculation. He would have slammed sideways into a pile of jagged junk if Jeeves hadn't popped into the gap and caught the giant dog with a manipulator field, gently lowering him back to the floor.

"I think Beowulf and I will pass on the mechanical bodies," Kelly said. "He doesn't need to jump any higher and I don't need to jump at all."

"But how are we going to get over all of this junk to the campsite?" Joe asked. "I don't see any passages, so I'm guessing we're supposed to put these things on and just wade through or climb over. Jeeves?"

"That was Libby's original idea," the Stryx said. "But I anticipated that one or more of you would balk at being shut up in a mobile sarcophagus, so I prepared another transportation option."

"You did?" Kelly asked. "As in, your idea, not Libby's? Maybe I'll take a look at the suit."

Beowulf whined and gave her a look that said, "Will you really throw your loyal dog off the troika to the wolves?" Kelly was forced to relent.

"Alright, Jeeves. How are you going to get the dog and I out of this metal wasteland?"

"Follow me," Jeeves said. He led them back in the direction from which he had first appeared. "Now just climb the stairs to the top and I'll float along-side."

"What stairs?" Kelly asked, surveying the mountain of junk.

Beowulf, having had his fill of leaping for the day, tentatively approached a horizontal metal member that struck him as unnaturally placed in the random pile of scrap. He put a paw on it to test the stability.

"That's right, Beowulf," Jeeves encouraged the dog. "One paw in front of the next. Show the ambassador how it's done."

Kelly looked again and saw a long series of stairs twisting their way up the surface of the mound. There was even a handrail, but it was welded together out of different pieces, with extra bits sticking out away from the treads, which effectively camouflaged the stairway. Actually, the effect was rather artistic.

"You built this yourself, Jeeves?" Kelly asked. She was somewhat impressed the Stryx would go to the trouble of getting the aesthetics right.

"I got Dring to help me," Jeeves admitted. "He wanted to come visit you anyway, and he's waiting on the other side."

The thought of seeing Dring was enough to get Kelly moving up the stairs behind Beowulf, who was already several steps above the deck and beginning to climb more rapidly. Despite its appearance, the handrail proved to be free of burrs and sharp edges, and she saw that the stairs were all carefully welded in place by expert hands.

"Joe," she called back over her shoulder. "You may as well get the kids moving over this stuff so we can set up camp. They can always come back and play in the junk piles later."

The exoskeleton suit Joe occupied lifted a hand in acknowledgement. When Kelly reached the top of the stairs, somewhat out of breath, she turned and saw six robotic figures picking their way over the scrap mounds.

For a second she thought the group was being chased by one of the original occupants of the deck, but then she remembered that Metoo was also encased in an exoskeleton. They were escorted by a floating Banger, who hadn't donned a suit, perhaps because he doubted his ability to count to infinity.

"Just climb in and pull down the safety bar," Jeeves said. Kelly delayed until the robotic figures disappeared over the crest of the scrap mountain range where it nearly reached the ceiling. Beowulf hopped into the front of the boxy vehicle, where he waited anxiously to get started so they could catch up with the rest of his pack. Kelly seated herself on the small bench and pulled the padded yoke down over her head and chest.

"Is this really necessary?" she asked Jeeves. "If you're going to carry us there, I trust you to do it without tipping the car over."

"Carry?" Jeeves said, and Kelly would have sworn that the immobile face of the exoskeleton suit the Stryx was wearing lifted an eyebrow. "That would violate the whole spirit of the thing. While Dring was welding, I carefully created a magnetized path to your destination, and believe you me, maintaining polarity in such a jumble is no easy task. I added a coil and an off-the-shelf magnetic levitation controller to the car so you can float there in style, though you'll never be more than a hand's breadth away from the surface."

"Oh, that sounds nice. But how does it go uphill?"

"Don't worry," Jeeves replied. "The magnetic repulsion and interlock is frictionless, so I just have to give you a good shove. At least, I think it will work, but we didn't have time to test it with a load."

"JEEVES!"

Kelly tried to lift the yoke, but it was locked in place, and she was suddenly flattened against the seatback by the acceleration of the power-assisted push-off. The cart started down the mound, gaining speed as it went, but bouncing like it was about to fly off into space at any second.

"J-E-E-E-E-E-E-V-V-E-S!" Kelly screamed, the sound rising and falling with the strong vibrations.

Beowulf curled up in his crash position and resolved to bite the Stryx trickster if he ever saw Jeeves in a form that wouldn't break a dog's teeth.

The cart slowed almost to a stop at the top of the next scrap hill, and Kelly saw her family working their way up the side of the adjacent mound. She waved frantically as the cart began to gain speed again, and then she saw that they were approaching an unlikely loop structure. She shut her eyes and screamed as the cart entered the loop and she found herself momentarily upside-down.

Five terrifying minutes later, the cart came to a halt, and she heard a click as her safety yoke released. Beowulf cautiously lifted his head, sniffed the air, and gingerly climbed out. Kelly waited another minute to make sure the cart wasn't going to start moving again, and then she followed the dog.

"Over here," Dring called. He was standing at a round table under a large umbrella that reminded her of a beachfront café on Earth where her parents had brought the family to vacation when she was a child. "I made you a pot of tea. Did you like my stairway?"

"Dring," Kelly replied shakily. "How could you conspire with Jeeves to scare me out of my wits? And I thought poor Beowulf was going to be sick."

"What was scary?" Dring asked. "I made the stairway perfectly stable, and I'm sure Jeeves wouldn't operate the roller coaster outside of the safety limitations. I'm looking forward to riding it myself."

"Roller coaster? He didn't say—I should have known he was up to something!"

"Did you like the loop? I sketched it out based on a memory of a roller coaster I rode on Horten Four many years ago."

"There was a roller coaster in the amusement park near the beach where my parents used to take us. By the time I was tall enough to go on it, they changed the admissions requirement to a minimum age of eighteen for insurance reasons, and kids couldn't ride even with parental consent."

"So this was your first time," Dring surmised. "You did very well. I only heard the one prolonged scream, assuming that was you and not the dog."

Beowulf gave the Maker a haughty stare, then turned and trotted off in the direction where he expected the rest of the family to appear.

"I don't get it, Dring. I thought Gryph was keeping all of these decks intact in case the owners reappeared or because the Stryx hate to throw away a garden, but there's nothing but scrap metal and assorted junk around here.

"Isn't it great? I've already gotten Gryph's permission to use whatever I want to create sculptures, and Jeeves asked me to work with him and Paul on extending the roller coaster so it goes all around the circumference of the deck. I've been thinking it would be fun to put a twist in the middle, like a Mobius strip, except riders would be upside-down for half of the route. Maybe that's why I've never seen it done before."

"But what if the original owners return and they don't like roller coasters?"

"The Plangers?" Dring asked in surprise. "But they died out long ago, the entire race. Miserable sentients, they made the Brupt look like sentimentalists by comparison. I suspect the only people who were sorry to see them go were the Alterians, since the Plangers went through fuel packs like crazy and never developed their own. They were accidental space-farers, now that I think about it. They were barely out of their stone age when a well-meaning species came along and gifted them with advanced technology. The Plangers just rushed from one labor-saving measure to the next, until they had nothing to do all day but sit around in their exoskeletons getting injected with recreational drugs."

Beowulf began to bark happily, and Kelly looked over to see her family starting down the last slope. Even with the mechanical assist from their robot suits, there was no way they could have traveled the same distance as her in that time. Clearly, the roller coaster had followed the long way around. She was going to give Jeeves a piece of her mind if he ever came out of hiding.

Twelve

"So whose bright idea was it to give a soapbox speech at the organics recycling center on a Saturday morning?" Shaina inquired. Walter and Daniel were both covered with spatters of rotten fruit and vegetables, and the HEEL organizer even had a wilted piece of lettuce peeking out from the breast pocket of his suit like a handkerchief.

"It was a directive from my boss," Walter explained. "Go where the people are. It made sense at the time."

"Speaking of time, you're lucky you arrived so late, Shaina, or you could have been covered in future compost as well," Daniel said, removing a bit of celery from behind his ear. "On the bright side, nobody throws away whole eggs, and the empty shells don't carry due to wind resistance."

"It's not luck, it's good housekeeping," she replied, displaying a plastic pail. "I stopped to pick-up Brinda's and my father's scraps as well. What did Walter say to get them so upset this time?"

"Oh, the usual thing," Daniel replied. "He was doing really well for a few minutes, people were stopping and listening, and there was even some applause. But then he got onto how we're all pampered pets that the Stryx are fattening for the kill, and I got a lesson in guilt by association."

"I thought you grew out of that," Shaina admonished Walter, sounding very much like a stern mother whose child keeps insisting that the neighbor girl has cooties.

"I did, but it was in the directive," Walter said sadly, surveying the damage to his suit. "Do you know a good dry cleaner?"

"Just ask our Stryx oppressors," Shaina replied tartly. "And didn't it occur to you that people who do their recycling on Saturday morning all have jobs, and that many of them would be offended by an accusation that they're charity cases? What's the deal with you anyway? The mystery woman from HEEL tells you to bash the Stryx and you bash the Stryx?"

"That's why I asked Daniel to come and record it for me," Walter said. "They want evidence that I'm working."

The junior consul held up a compact immersive-quality mobile camera that Shaina hadn't noticed amidst the overall tossed-salad effect of their appearance. There was a white substance that looked like mayonnaise on the lens.

"I hope that's not a rental," she said.

"HEEL sent it for recording my appearances," Walter explained. "It's all time-stamped, of course, so it gives them a way to check up on me. That's why I figured I better put in the talking points they insist on. It's my first job outside of student teaching, you know. I'd always heard that things were tougher in the real world, but I didn't think it would be this hard. Whatever happened to free speech?"

"Well, there's no point in standing around here looking like yesterday's lunch," Shaina told them. "Clive pinged me earlier and asked that I bring you both into his office for a chat."

"Are you an EarthCent Intelligence agent too?" Walter asked.

"Part-time," Shaina admitted. "It fits in with the auction circuit and I get free access to the business intelligence. We used to pay for a subscription to their all-species bankruptcy listings to receive leads for auction merchandise."

"How about we all meet at InstaSitter in fifteen minutes?" Daniel suggested.

"He means EarthCent Intelligence," Shaina explained to Walter. "It's his favorite bad joke."

"I may be a little late since I want to drop off my suit," Walter said. "I wonder if HEEL will reimburse me for the cleaning?"

"I don't know about that, but I just subvoced Libby and she says there's a dry cleaner in the Little Apple," Daniel said. "I guess it made sense to locate in the middle of the restaurant district and catch people while they're thinking about it, before the stain sets in."

"Alright. I still have to dump my stuff, unless one of you rebels-without-a-brain wants another dose." Shaina brandished her bucket in a mock-threatening manner, and the men headed off to their quarters to clean up.

Forty minutes later they were back together, sitting around the display desk in EarthCent Intelligence's conference room. Thomas was present, along with Clive and Blythe, and Jeeves had floated in as well, though nobody was quite sure who had invited him.

"You have a good eye for framing the action." Blythe offered this compliment to Daniel after the recording of Walter's performance came to an abrupt halt with the impact of a half-eaten tuna salad sandwich, heavy on the mayo, against the lens.

"It helps that he gestures a lot while he speaks," Daniel replied. "I could almost see the weight of the EarthCent dictatorship crushing us all into the dust before the food started flying."

"Is it possible that your employers are trying to get you killed so they don't have to pay you?" Thomas asked the deeply chagrined HEEL organizer.

"Don't be too hard on Walter," Clive said. "Our cultural attachés have been reporting similar speeches being given at every station on the tunnel network. We also have confirmation from Operation Honeymoon that the same thing is happening on the open worlds."

"Which makes you wonder who is paying for all of this," Blythe continued her husband's thought. "Why plunk down the amount of creds involved here, and then proceed with the naiveté of a student movement challenging the administration to change the lunch menu to all desserts?"

"I thought that sending the camera and demanding proof-of-performance with a list of talking points was a major step-up in professionalism," Daniel said. "It's their platform that's the problem. Most humans are open to talking about self-government, at least until you get to the part about taxes. But people react badly when you tell them that they're stooges and that their benefactors, the Stryx, are secretly plotting their demise."

"I could be secretly plotting," Jeeves contributed. Everybody ignored him.

"Whoever is running HEEL must know that the message isn't working by now," Clive said. "Don't you submit reports, Walter?"

"Sure, but I got back a copy of my employment agreement with the section about adhering to the organization's platform circled in red. And there was another holo-cube course, apparently an update to the last one."

"A new twist on multi-level grassroots organizing?" Shaina asked.

"I haven't played it yet. The package showed up this morning just as I was heading out, but I brought the first couple cubes in case you want to watch. There's something about this whole thing that makes me think it's better to have witnesses."

"Fire away," Clive told him.

Walter reached in his pocket and pulled out a holo-cube. He looked around for something to throw it against before settling on the ceiling. Apparently he didn't put enough muscle into the toss because the cube bounced off without releasing the holo-recording. Jeeves fielded it and crushed the cube in his pincer.

"Welcome to the Human Expatriates Election League orientation course, revision A," the beautiful masked woman addressed them from the hologram. "If you watched the previous version of this series, please forget it, and destroy any unopened cubes by boiling them in water until they dissolve."

"I bet she tells you to drink the water," Blythe interjected rapidly.

"The water can be used for hot beverages or as stock for a nutritious soup," the instructor continued. "Remember, an army marches on its stomach." Her head and shoulders began shifting from side to side, and the cameras zoomed out, showing that she was marching in place.

Walter slouched in his chair and Daniel patted him on the back sympathetically. The cameras continued to pull back, and the hologram now showed tens, then hundreds, then thousands of animated figures marching in lock-step with the instructor. There was an awkward splice, after which the hologram picked up with the second half of the content from the previous first cube of the series.

"That was...different," Shaina commented. "Shall we go for two?"

Walter reluctantly dug another cube out of his pocket, checked the number, and passed it to Jeeves. Before the Stryx crushed the cube, he turned it over, observing the markings. He seemed to hesitate for a moment, holding it up to the light, an action he surely didn't need to perform given the suite of built-in sensors at his command.

"Can you tell who manufactured it?" Clive asked, catching on that the Stryx was trying to hint at something.

"The Hortens are the only manufacturers of one-shot holo-cubes on the tunnel network. Economies of scale and all that," Jeeves replied. "Some of the advanced species can reverse-engineer the spent crystals to trace the recording, but I'm sure you knew that already or I wouldn't have mentioned it."

"You mean it's not just a concentrated cube of light and sound that disperses as it plays?" Shaina asked.

"Holo-cubes are made from a packed matrix of micro-scopic crystals," Jeeves said. "Of course, they're almost indistinguishable from common dust once they've given up their energy, and merely blowing on them would disperse the crystals over such a wide area as to render collecting enough to analyze a difficult task."

Blythe looked at Jeeves speculatively and then slid him her empty coffee mug. The Stryx held the holo-cube just above the rim and squeezed.

"Welcome back to the HEEL course in multi-level or-ganizing," the beautiful instructor said. It appeared to be the same recording they had watched the previous week, with the action taking place in an outdoor market, crowded with crude animations of pedestrians and merchandise hawkers.

"Just watch how it works as I start to recruit downliners," she continued on script. "Let's begin with him."

Her first victim was still dressed in a Victorian suit that could have been from the wardrobe of one of Kelly's favorite authors, and he again halted in front of their instructor and waited. This time the splice was only detectable because the gentlemen's blink stopped halfway and started again.

"Would you like to earn extra money while working for human self-government?"

"With all of my heart," the man replied.

"And what would you say if I offered you ten millicreds a month for each person you signed up, plus five millicreds for each person they signed up?" the instructor continued.

"God save the King, I'll do it," the animated figure declared.

"Here's a hundred creds on account," the beautiful woman said, handing the gentlemen a cartoonish bag of coins. "Keep careful records or your local HEEL organizer won't be able to disburse future payments."

A gold line popped into existence between the woman and her paid activist. The man quickly purchased the loyalty of another passerby, and a green line was established between the two. The hologram sped up, and the space above the conference table rapidly filled with multicolored lines. Finally, the cameras zoomed back in on the masked woman, who gathered all of the gold lines in her hands and pulled. All of the people in the marketplace fell flat on their faces.

"I'm ready for the election," she said cheerfully. "In the next cube, I'll show you how to convince your paid supporters that they are choosing you of their own free will." The hologram dissolved.

"I quit!" Walter howled. "This is worse than going to graduate school and being forced to pretend that I agreed with everybody's conflicting theories about non-events, all for a lousy stipend."

Blythe put a saucer on top of her coffee mug and then she placed the assembly on the sideboard for safe keeping. Later she could ask Tinka to send it to Herl for analysis.

"I really wanted to give HEEL the benefit of the doubt, but they do seem a bit nefarious," Daniel said. "If their idea of self-government is bribing people to vote for their paymasters, I don't see how EarthCent can support their call for free elections."

"Funny, but I was thinking just the opposite." Clive said. He winked at his wife. Blythe flashed him a look of comprehension and began to fish around in the drawer of the sideboard. Whatever she was searching for was buried by a variety of bottle openers, stirrers, disposable chopsticks, and lots of take-out packages of ketchup, mustard and duck sauce. "I'm convinced that you're a good guy, Walter, and I respect a man who quits a job over ethical considerations. But what if you could do the right thing and earn twice as much as you're making now?"

"That doesn't sound possible," Walter replied. The sudden grins of his companions made him suspicious he was being set up as the butt of some insider joke. Blythe returned to the table and dropped something right in front of the former HEEL organizer.

Walter looked down at the button and read, "I'm a double agent for the humans."

"You'll keep drawing your salary and expenses from HEEL, and we'll match it," Clive told him. "I wouldn't have interfered with a genuine self-government movement whether I agreed with it or not, but there's something going on here that needs to be investigated."

"But even if I wanted to do it, I don't know anything," Walter protested. "It's like being an undergrad again. I get my marching orders from on high, and now they even require video evidence that I'm toeing the line."

"I see it as a classic two-way operation," Thomas said. "Disinformation in, information out. We need to turn Walter into HEEL's top organizer."

"Agreed," Blythe said, and the EarthCent Intelligence crew began discussing their potential new asset as if he weren't in the room. "Walter does a pretty good job with the public speaking, but as soon as he begins telling people what they don't want to hear, he loses them."

"Even the best salesmen have trouble selling something they can't make themselves believe in," Shaina pointed out.

"Maybe you could hypnotize him," Jeeves offered helpfully. "I saw it in one of your old movies."

"I think Clive has something much simpler in mind," Daniel said, observing that the director of EarthCent Intelligence was sporting a grin like the cat that just swallowed the canary.

"What about it, Walter?" Clive asked. "Are you onboard? All we ask is that you do your best for humanity."

"I don't know anything about being a spy," Walter said, toying with the button. "We looked down on all that stuff in school."

"I've got room in the training class if you want to come," Thomas offered. "One of our candidates dropped out during first aid training. I guess she couldn't stomach it."

"Were you doing gross training scenarios with fake blood and broken limbs?" Shaina asked.

"Not at all," Thomas replied defensively. "We had just finished with emergency reboots and Chance was demonstrating how you can do field repairs to skin with a special two-part epoxy the Sharf make. They put the same stuff in lifeboats for in case there's a meteor breech."

"You were going to put epoxy on the poor woman?" Daniel asked.

"Not on her, on me," Thomas replied in frustration. "One of the deficiencies in the training program Joe and Woojin put together is that it's so human-centric. If Chance or I ever lead a mission into hostile territory, it would be nice to think that at least a few of our fellow agents could deal with a simple skin rupture. It's not like artificial people can heal themselves, you know, and these bodies are expensive."

Thirteen

"It's a good thing we're traveling on the expense account because it's going to cost a fortune in fuel to get off of this big rock," Lynx complained to her husband. They had just exited the Prudence on the Verlock world of Fyndal and the gravity made her feel as if she had gained ten or twenty pounds overnight. "Oh, no. You hear that pump whining? Prudence can't raise her ramp in this gravity."

Woojin turned back to the ship and saw that the ramp of Lynx's two-man trader was trembling and hesitating. Then it gave up with a hydraulic sigh and sank back down to the ground.

"What do you have for a manual bypass on this ship?" Woojin asked, examining the ramp.

"I'm looking at him," Lynx replied pointedly.

Woojin shook his head in mock despair, crouched down like a weight lifter preparing to clean and jerk, and worked his fingers under the end of the ramp. At first it barely budged, but then the ramp began moving upwards, the speed directly proportional to the amount of blood swelling the veins in the straining man's face and neck. By the time he had it chest-high and shifted his hands to push from the bottom, the center of gravity of the ramp had moved inwards enough that the hydraulic pistons were able to handle the load.

"Lynx marry strong man," he said, thumping his chest in imitation of the actor in the twentieth remake of Tarzan which they had watched the previous day in the tunnel. Then he made the mistake of pursing his lips like an ape who expected a kiss for his troubles.

"Save it for Jane," Lynx dismissed him curtly. She scanned the tarmac for signs of activity, but no vehicles or people were in sight. "Did I hear wrong over the comm or did they promise to have somebody come and meet us? I'd hate to have to hike all the way to that terminal carrying this extra weight."

"Gravity is only about ten percent above nominal here. Humans wouldn't willingly settle on a world where it's a lot higher. There are too many health complications in the long term, especially on the heart and with pregnancy."

"How come the whole time we were dating I never heard you mention pregnancy once, and now that we're married, it's in every other sentence out of your mouth?"

"You're exaggerating, as usual," Woojin said, brushing the dust off his hands. "Look, here comes our ride."

"An ox cart?" Lynx asked in disbelief. "The Verlocks are one of the most advanced species on the tunnel network. Good grief. It will take that thing twenty minutes to get here."

"Do you want to wait or walk to meet them?"

"Wait," she replied, and began looking around for something to sit down on. The only nearby objects on the tarmac were her ship and her husband. "Or, we could walk to meet them."

"Whoa!" the burly driver called to his beasts, when the two parties finally met halfway between Lynx's ship and the terminal building.

"Hello, friend," Woojin said in greeting. "I'm Pyun Woojin and this is my wife Lynx. We spoke with administrator Hep a few hours ago, and he said somebody would be out for us."

"That's - me," the driver said, pausing strangely between his words as if English wasn't his natural language. "Welcome - aboard."

The honeymoon couple carefully climbed into the old-fashioned transport which they could now see was carved out of a giant stone. The wheels were also stone, as were the unpadded benches. The driver flicked the leads and the oxen began the long walk back to their stable.

"I didn't catch your name," Woojin said, trying to strike up a conversation with the taciturn driver.

"Ner," the man grunted after a pause, as if the single syllable required a special effort.

"Ner," Woojin repeated, offering his hand to the driver. "Interesting vehicle you have here. I've never had a ride in a stone cart before."

Ner looked at Woojin's hand for a moment as if he was puzzled by the ancient human greeting, and then he slowly reached over and clasped it. The ex-mercenary was impressed by the driver's strong leathery grip.

"Stone - doesn't – rust – and – resists – acid - rain," Ner said, proving he was fluent in English after all.

"Isn't it incredibly heavy for the poor oxen?" Lynx asked.

"Weighs – less – than - us. Verlock – skimmer - technology. Wheels – for - show."

"This thing can fly but you're using oxen to pull it around?"

"My – oxen – get - airsick," Ner said, and then his mouth opened wide and he began to laugh with a deep heaving sound, "Hah – Hah - Hah."

Despite the lava-like delivery, it took Woojin and Lynx a few seconds to get the joke, but Ner gave them plenty of time to join in.

"Alright, I'll bite," Lynx said after they all stopped laughing. "Why use oxen at all?"

"For - guests," Ner explained. "Ceremonial - occasion."

"Oh. Thank you."

"Second – time – this - month," the driver added, or maybe he had never stopped talking and Lynx's reply had fallen during one of his pauses.

"So the hours are good. How about the pay?" Woojin asked in jest.

"Hah - Hah. The – hours – are – very - good," Ner agreed. "It's – lucky – I – have – a – paying – hobby – for – my – free - time."

"What's that," Lynx inquired.

"Mathematician – third - rank," Ner replied modestly. "Hep – is – our – only – first – rank - mathematician. The – Verlocks – invite – him – to – lecture – in – their - academies."

"I wondered how humans ended up living on a Verlock world, and one with high gravity to boot," Lynx said. "You're all mathematicians."

"Not - all," Ner corrected her. "Some – are - mages. Verlocks – know – words – of - power. Whoa - there."

The oxen responded to the driver's cry and halted in front of the terminal building.

"It – was – nice – to – meet - you," Ner said. "My – daughter – waits - inside – to – bring – you – to – the - academy."

147

The small terminal building only had the one door and it slid open at their approach. Just as Ner had promised, an athletic teenage girl was waiting to greet them.

"Hi. You must be Lynx and Woojin," she said. "I'm Tac, and I'll be your guide."

"Tac, what a relief you speak at a normal speed," Lynx replied. "Your father was very nice, but he talks like a..."

"Like a Verlock," Tac finished Lynx's sentence. "All of our parents do that now. Who knows, maybe I'll slow down when I get older, but I don't really see the benefit. Talking slow at home isn't a useful skill, like, say, sculpting."

"Are you a sculptor?"

"Everybody is on Fyndal. Sculpture and math, that's why we're here. Well, a little bit of magic, but not many humans have the aptitude to become a mage."

Tac led the visitors to an elevator as she spoke, and the car began descending as soon as the three entered.

"Implant controlled?" Woojin asked.

Tac looked at him oddly.

"The elevator. It started as soon as we entered and you didn't have to push any buttons or tell it where to go."

"Oh, I get it," she said. "No, we don't use implants here. The controller detects people entering the elevator and it only has the one destination."

"The academy?"

"The subway," Tac replied. "We mainly live underground on Fyndal. Human lungs aren't equipped to deal with all of the dust and sulfur in the atmosphere. There's an enormous canyon not too far from the spaceport terminal where we filter the atmosphere and keep the herds."

"Just how large is the human community here?"

Tac made an elaborate hand gesture, something like sculpting an invisible ball out of clay and then tossing it upwards.

"It's unlucky to count sentients," she said, after performing the Verlock cleansing ritual. "We're about the only thing we don't count. I can tell you that the dining services provided just under thirty thousand lunches today," she added slyly.

"And you live side by side with the Verlocks?" Woojin asked.

"Oh, no. They like it too hot, and they're so bulky and move so slowly that we'd get stuck behind them in narrow passages all of the time. Some of our parents move kind of slowly too, but that's more age and gravity than anything else."

"So the grown-ups imitate the Verlocks but the kids do their own thing?" Lynx inquired.

"Imitate? Oh, you mean the slow speaking. It's just that our parents learned Verlock when they were adults. It's such a powerful language, especially with the slow pacing, that it sort of rewired their brains. I started learning when I was seven so I'm native bilingual and it's easy for me to switch back and forth. It's the same with all my friends and their families."

"I can see we're going to have a long conversation with Mr. Hep," Woojin commented.

"Hep still speaks normally," Tac said. "They say he learned the language from a Stryx librarian when he was growing up. Then he impersonated a Verlock kid on a station in order to take their correspondence courses in math."

The elevator came to a halt and their weight returned to normal, or ten percent above normal. They exited onto a brightly lit platform in front of a trench that was paved with odd ceramic tiles.

"Magnetic monopoles," Tac explained, pointing at the ceramic tiles like a professional tour guide. "The Verlocks synthesize them at the elementary particle level and lock them into ceramic substrates. There's a limit to the density, of course, but they get enough field strength to levitate a decent train without the need for an external current supply."

"Don't tell me," Woojin said. "You pull the train with oxen."

"The cars run on a continuous cable loop," the girl replied straight-faced. "The oxen prefer to ride underground."

There was a restrained squealing sound as a low-slung train car that reminded Lynx of something from an old movie pulled into the station and stopped.

"There's no hurry, it will wait as long as there are people on the platform," Tac told them. "Look up above it. Do you see the clamp thing on the cables? The cable nearest to us is always moving through the tunnel, and the other one is the brake cable, which only runs for the length of the platform. When the car enters the station, it shifts its clamp from the tow cable to the brake cable."

"What holds the moving cable suspended up there?" Woojin inquired, squinting against the lights.

"Magnets," the girl replied. "The Verlocks do all sorts of neat things with magnetic fields. Some of their worlds use a moon with an iron core deliberately placed in a low orbit around the planet to generate electricity."

"Wouldn't that result in a tremendous amount of atmospheric lightning?" Woojin asked, trying to picture how the system could work.

"Oh, yes," Tac replied enthusiastically. "The Verlocks love lightning."

After the three humans entered the car, it shifted its clamp and began to accelerate gently. Lynx plunked herself down on a bench and immediately regretted that she hadn't sat in a more controlled manner. The benches were stone.

"Next stop, Bath," an artificial voice intoned.

"The Verlocks make fun of us for cooling the water in our hot springs and filtering out some of the chemicals," Tac told them conversationally. "Personally, I'm not interested in tanning my skin while it's still attached to my body."

"Tanning? Oh, you mean, like leather," Lynx said.

"Yes, I forgot that some humans use the same word for exposing themselves to the sun to darken their skin," the girl replied. "The Verlocks intentionally tan their own skins to toughen them up for volcanic environments, starting when they're babies. You could dissolve plastics in the baths they like to soak in."

"Bath," the artificial voice repeated, and the car came to a gentle halt. A party of noisy kids wearing towels and flip-flops got on, and the subway started out again. "Next stop, Academy."

"How do the humans here generate the money to pay for all of this?" Lynx asked the girl.

"All of our parents are on scholarships," Tac explained, looking a bit embarrassed. "I think it's some kind of experiment the Verlocks are running, but my friends who were born on stations think that the Stryx are paying for the whole thing. They say that the 'Ask an Alien' show proved it."

"So the Grenouthians must have already broadcast Kelly's interview with Srythlan," Woojin commented. "How was it?"

"Brilliant!" Tac said enthusiastically. "I learned more about Verlock history in an hour than I have in the eight years we've been living here. They aren't secretive, but they think that saying anything about their own achievements is the same as bragging. I've tried reading some of their history books, but they explain everything in terms of math and I'm not advanced enough to follow the proofs yet. Oh, and the EarthCent ambassador who asked the questions was so funny. We couldn't stop laughing."

"I'll tell her when we get back," Woojin promised.

"Academy," the artificial voice announced as the subway car slowed to a halt.

"Oh, wow. Hep came himself to meet you," Tac said, making it clear that the visitors should consider themselves greatly honored.

A young man with a receding hairline who looked to be about twenty-five years old waited for them on the platform. Tac led the guests directly over and they made their mutual introductions.

"I can't tell you how happy I am to see you," Hep said, looking keenly at the couple. "We have a problem that defies our attempts at a solution, and my Verlock mentor suggested fighting fire with fire."

"We're fire?" Woojin guessed.

"You're from off-world and so is our problem," Hep explained. "Have you ever heard of something called the Human Expatriates Election League?"

"HEEL," Lynx answered in disgust. "We've been stumbling across their tracks all through our honeymoon. When we reported in after leaving Two Mountains, we received a new itinerary rerouting us in your direction. You placed an ad on a mercenary recruitment board looking for temporary police help?"

"We really don't know what to do with the young woman in question, though there have been some surprisingly violent suggestions," Hep continued. "Very un-Verlock-like. She arrived three weeks ago on a tramp trader which departed immediately after she disembarked. We should have known there was a problem right then."

"What's she been doing that has you so upset?" Woojin asked.

"She's interfering with our academy," Hep explained. "She bursts into our lecture halls and makes speeches about free elections and the will of the people. The worst part is that she keeps trying to promote a scheme where we sell each other our votes and become rich. The math doesn't work at all, it defies logic. She's already ruined two interactive blackboards by drawing stick figures and lines all over them with indelible markers."

"Have you asked her to leave?" Lynx inquired.

"Approximately a hundred time a day. She just keeps on talking, and most of our scholars have an acquired speech impediment of sorts so they can't get a word in edgewise. The only thing that slows her down is an argument, and I'm the only adult in the community who can match her pace. I've been wasting all of my time chasing her around and debating in hallways so she won't disrupt the lectures."

"And you'd like us to...?"

"Arrest her. Take her home with you. Sell her to Farlings as a laboratory test subject. Just as long as you get her out of here!"

"If you're the official government, I don't mind filling in as the temporary police force," Woojin said. "Just deputize me and point me to the lady in question and I'll take her into custody."

"And then?" Lynx demanded.

"Well, we'll have to take her with us."

"On MY two-man trader? On MY honeymoon?"

"Ooh, that is kind of rough," Tac said sympathetically.

"We have a lifeboat, don't we?" Woojin asked, in an infuriatingly calm manner.

"And guess who's going to be sleeping in it from now on," Lynx replied acidly.

"And the lifeboat has an emergency stasis pod," Woojin added. There was a long pause while Lynx thought it over.

"Not bad," she said. "How are we going to get the HEEL into it?"

"I always start by asking nicely," the ex-mercenary explained. "Then I outline the alternatives, and if that doesn't work, the options range from a wrestling match to a tranquilizer dart."

"What's this woman look like?" Lynx asked their hosts.

"Twenty-something, attractive," Hep replied.

"She looks like a fashion model," Tac said.

"Call your dad and tell him not to unyoke the oxen," Lynx instructed the teenager. "We're going back to my ship for a tranquilizer gun, assuming my husband actually brought such a thing on my honeymoon."

"Our honeymoon," Woojin corrected her with a grin. "I thought I might need it for protection since you're obviously so crazy about me."

Fourteen

"Come right this way, please. Oh, I am so happy to see you. We haven't had any new employees in such a long time. Let's see if I can even remember what to do. Well, first we'll need to fix you up with some IDs."

"Uh, we may have gotten off on the wrong deck," Kelly said. The plastic features of the bubbly android collapsed in hurt disbelief, making the ambassador hope that it wasn't a mistake after all. "Banger? Can you check with Libby?"

"There's no mistake, Ambassador," the little Stryx replied. "We're the new temporary employees starting today," he added, for the benefit of the reception android.

"Of course, of course. All of the employees are temps, except me, that is," the android replied. "You gave me a scare there. I've spent weeks getting everything ready. Let's see, now. Party of seven?"

Beowulf growled from deep in his chest.

"I'm sorry, eight. Always room for another employee. Follow me, now. Follow me."

The android turned abruptly and hustled off down a long corridor between what looked like tiny square offices, all without doors. Joe tried a quick calculation as to how many cubicles the deck might contain if it ran the whole length of Union Station. After squaring his guess at the radius and multiplying by pi, the number was so large that it made him uncomfortable.

"Here we are, here we are. One at a time now. Stand in front of the blue curtain and speak your name. Come on now, don't be shy."

Dorothy stepped in front of the blue curtain. She faced the android, which had moved behind a device that was obviously some sort of camera, and said, "Dorothy McAllister."

"Perfect. Lovely teeth. I can see you won't be running up the cost of our dental plan," the android gushed. There was a sound like a vending machine disgorging a very thin candy bar, and the receptionist handed over a picture of Dorothy encased in heavy plastic, threaded with a silk lanyard for hanging around the neck. Her name was neatly printed under the picture. "Next, please."

Mist stepped forward and identified herself, followed by Samuel, Ailia and Banger. Joe went next, and Kelly, who hadn't been expecting a picture that morning and was trying to do something with her hair, nodded at Beowulf to jump in front of her. The dog decided on the spot that a contraction of his name would save space on the badge for what would no doubt be an impressive job title. He settled on "Wulf," though somehow the obsolete alien technology interpreted it as "Woof." Kelly went last, feeling self-conscious.

"Now we need to assign your jobs. Let's see if I can re-member how to do this," the android said. "Please, line up there, and those IDs are for wearing, not playing with, young man. Alright, the tallest person in the room is always the leader." Twin beams of light shot out of the android's eyes, and Joe's badge now identified him as "President."

"You look like a customer relations manager to me," the android told Kelly, and in a flash, it was on her ID. Mist and Dorothy found themselves assigned to research and development, Samuel, Ailia and Banger were all identified as quality control testers, and Beowulf was placed in charge of security.

"Is there anybody else working here?" Kelly asked hesitantly. She didn't want to hurt the android's feelings again, but she was a little suspicious of a company where the receptionist doubled as the head of human resources.

"You'll be interacting with the other employees as soon as you enter your assigned offices. I've prepared a special block so you can be close together because I know how hard it can be to settle into a new job."

The android led them out of the photo ID room and down a different corridor, where both Kelly and Joe made it a point to peek into each cubicle they passed. All were immaculately clean and decidedly empty. Beowulf was for once pleased with the lack of strange scents on the deck. It would make security a breeze.

"Here we are, now. Here we are. You can choose from any of these offices here. Just press your ID against the blank nameplate and it will copy your information and customize all of the equipment interfaces. Once you've done that, you'll find that the arrow on the back of your badge serves as a compass that will always lead you back to your office so you can't get lost. We had a bit of a problem with that in the early days."

"We just go in our cubicles, then?" Joe asked.

"You start by selecting your office," the android replied testily. It seemed determined to insist on using the grandiose term for the tiny spaces with fabric walls. "After that, well, you're the president."

Dorothy and Mist held a brief whispered consultation before choosing their side-by-side cubicles. Banger, Samuel and Ailia took three adjacent cubicles across the corridor, and Kelly and Joe claimed two cubicles next to the teenage girls. Beowulf was a little more selective, entering and leaving a number of cubicles before selecting a larger one that included a conference table under which he could nap. It didn't have a nameplate he could program, but as head of security, he decided to make an exception for himself.

The bustling android disappeared as soon as the new employees entered their cubicles, and the ceiling lights above all of the surrounding spaces dimmed to what one might expect from emergency lighting. Inside the occupied cubicles, holo-displays lit up, though Beowulf didn't see his as it was above the roof of his improvised cave.

"Did you just get a calendar on your display, Kel?" Joe called. His voice sounded a bit deadened by the walls of the cubicle and it occurred to him that there might be an audio suppression field as well. He was about to get up and go to her when he noticed a screen pad on the arm of his office chair with seven icons, each showing the face of one of his "employees". He tapped his wife's face softly.

"Kel?"

"Hello?" Her voice seemed to come from everywhere and nowhere, rather like Libby sounded in wide-open spaces. "How did you do that, Joe?"

"There's a screen with all of your faces on the arm of my chair," Joe replied.

"Oh, I see," Kelly said. "Wait, I only have six. I don't get to call you?"

"Well, I am president." There wasn't a response because Kelly had discovered how to break the connection. Joe sighed and rose to his feet to go and apologize. He stuck his head into his son's cubicle across the corridor to see how Samuel was getting along, and saw that the boy's holo-display was split into four cubes. Three cubes were given over to a conference between the young quality control testers, and the fourth cube seemed to hold the contents of a toy chest.

"That's the one I want to test," Samuel said, touching an improbable-looking weapon that likely shot a stream of water. Joe withdrew and stepped into Kelly's cubicle.

"You don't knock?" she inquired. "I thought we were keeping relations on a professional basis."

"Come on, Kel. I was just kidding about pulling rank."

"That doesn't put your face on my armrest."

"Well, I should be able to change that. I am president after all."

"If you think I'm—what was that?" Kelly asked, breaking off her complaint as something silently flashed by behind Joe's back.

The president stuck his head back out into the corridor and saw a delivery bot setting down a package in front of Samuel's cubicle opening. Ailia was already outside her cubicle picking up a rainbow-colored stuffed animal of some sort, and the delivery bot then proceeded to hand an abacus to Banger, who met him in the corridor.

"Product delivery for our quality control testers," Joe said over his shoulder. "I saw Samuel picking out what I think was a water gun, Ailia must have chosen the stuffed animal, and Banger has one of those old-fashioned calculators that use beads."

"So it's serious? They're going to test the products?" Kelly stuck her head out behind Joe to see if he was making things up, then jerked back just in time to avoid being hit by a stream of water.

"I don't think it's a good idea to shoot that thing in the corridor," Joe said in irritation, wiping his face on his sleeve.

"But it's my job!" Samuel protested.

"Don't make me call security," Joe warned.

"Awww." Samuel let the gun fall to parade rest.

"Maybe there's a special room for quality control testing," Kelly suggested. "I'd ask somebody, but I don't see how. Where are the other employees our one-android reception committee told us about?" She looked again at the display pad on her armchair, while Joe scanned the cubicle for signs of communications devices.

"Mr. McAllister? Mrs. McAllister? Is there something I can help you with?"

An android which bore a conspicuous resemblance to the one who had welcomed them to work appeared at the opening of Kelly's cubicle.

"Do you know if there's a space where the children can play with their new toys?" Kelly inquired.

The android tilted its head to the side like a puzzled dog.

"Our quality control team needs some lab space to test products," Joe said.

"Oh yes, of course. You can choose any space you think is appropriate, Mr. McAllister. This area of the company is a bit underutilized at present. Is there anything else?"

"How did you know we needed something?" Kelly asked.

"I was dispatched by the board of directors," the android replied, looking a bit embarrassed. "Was there anything else?"

"That will do it," Joe said, shaking his head at his wife to discourage further inquiries. Kelly looked at him questioningly, and he mouthed, "Libby."

"Why don't you take the children and see if you can find a good place nearby for them to play, I mean work, and I'll keep an eye on the girls," Kelly said. If the company they were employed by was being directly operated by the Stryx, as Joe suggested, it couldn't hurt to go along with the fun until dinner anyway.

While Joe took the young quality control testers in search of lab space, Kelly checked up on the teens. They had already mastered the interactive holo-display sufficiently to be hard at work collaborating on a new fashion line, which from the look of the accessories, would be marketed exclusively to princesses. Kelly was about to join in the fun when the android appeared yet again and tapped her on the shoulder.

"You're needed in your office, Mrs. McAllister," the android murmured politely.

"Oh, I'll be right there," Kelly said. The moment she settled into her chair, the holo-display lit up with the face of the Jill-of-all-trades android.

"There's been a problem with a large shipment of widgets to an important customer," the android said. "It appears to have gone missing from the warehouse."

"Uh, what are the widgets and who is the customer?" Kelly asked, trying to enter into the spirit of the thing.

"Don't you want to call a meeting with the president and security chief?" the android suggested, ignoring her question.

"Oh, I could do that," Kelly said. "Wait, I don't have the president on my call thingy."

"Hold on a minute, I'll put you through to his secretary," the android replied. The background color on the holo-display changed, but the same android remained in the foreground. "President's office."

"Aren't you the same..." Kelly's voice trailed off when she saw the pained expression on the android's face. "Uh, I'd like to schedule a meeting with the president and the head of security."

"The president is out of his office right now, but I can contact Mr. Woof and arrange for a meeting in one hour," the android replied happily.

"Could I ask you..." Kelly began, but when she saw the nervous expression on the android's face, she changed her mind. "Forget it. But is there an official history of the company available? As the customer relations manager, I think that understanding our past would help me, er, relate to our customers."

"Excellent idea," the android said. "The board of directors has approved your request and that information will be made available immediately."

Kelly spent the next hour flipping through the virtual pages that described the founding and early years of "The Company," which seemed to be its only official designation. It was started by a vaguely humanoid species with orange skin and too many eyes, long before the Drazens or the Hortens had joined the tunnel network. The company was vertically integrated, owning everything from the supply chain to retail outlets, and it seemed to have manufactured and sold just about everything imaginable at one time or another.

A cheerful android face suddenly replaced the virtual pages on her holo-display. "Time for your meeting," the president's secretary chirped. "Just follow the arrow on the back of your ID."

Kelly stood up and flipped her ID over on its lanyard, placing it on her palm. The arrow pointed through the cubicle's wall toward Joe's office, functioning like a compass rather than a navigation system. Instead of climbing the partition, she stepped out into the corridor and checked quickly to make sure that Dorothy and Mist hadn't vanished. The girls were busy adding jewels to their line of ball gowns. Then she walked into Joe's office, intentionally neglecting to knock, but it was empty.

The ambassador went back into the corridor and tried following the arrow on the back of her ID as closely as possible. It was clearly pointing to a space beyond Joe's cubicle in the same row, so she continued along until the arrow pointed directly into an opening. Joe and Beowulf were already waiting for her at the table.

"What are the kids doing?" Kelly asked.

"Our quality control testers will be in their lab until supper, which will happen as soon as Stanley and Donna arrive with our food," Joe replied. "Samuel rejected the gun on the principle that it ran out of ammunition, and Ailia concluded that her stuffed animal was insufficiently water-proofed. When I left, they had moved on to testing an alien game that involved colorful floating balls that knock into each other, sort of like billiards without the cues or table. Banger was keeping score on his abacus."

"Alright," Kelly said. "You're obviously having a good time being the president but now it's time to deal with business. Do you want the good news first or the bad news?"

"The bad news," Joe replied without hesitation.

"An order of widgets for one of our best customers has gone missing from the warehouse."

Beowulf's ears perked up. Warehouse thieves? He'd sniff them out if the trail was still fresh. But where exactly was the warehouse?

"Do we have any more details?" Joe asked.

"Well, that's the good news, sort of. I've been reading through the company history, and as near as I can tell, it was set up to provide busywork by a species that had gone overboard on automation and accidentally created a zero-employment economy."

"So rather than selling stuff to real customers, they steal it from their own warehouse?" Joe guessed.

"It's much more complicated than that. Did you ever hear the story about the two sailors shipwrecked on a desert island who both became wealthy by selling each other seashells on credit?"

"I think you just told it to me, unless you left something out."

"It's like the advanced species version of that. They created this company to employ all of the members of their species who wanted jobs, but their actual product was keeping each other busy."

"Why didn't they make real products and sell them to real customers if they wanted to work?"

"Because their automation could do it cheaper and faster, and they didn't think it was logical to shut it all down. So they came in to work every day, designed prototypes, tested them, manufactured and warehoused them, then recycled the inventory into feedstock for the next cycle. And they spent lots of time having meetings."

The economic logic made no sense to Beowulf, but he did gather that nothing had really been stolen and that there weren't any criminals to track down. He stopped paying attention and went back to thinking about food. The Huravian hound's sense memory was so good that he found himself drooling over the imagined smell of Donna's casserole.

"Knock, knock," the embassy office manager said, entering the conference room. "Are we interrupting an important meeting?"

"I thought I heard something about a closed-cycle company," Stanley added, setting a large picnic basket on the conference table. "You know they were quite common on Earth before the Stryx opened the planet."

"But you're always telling us that Earth was going broke," Kelly objected. "Doesn't running a company that doesn't really sell anything cost a lot of money?"

"Sure," Stanley replied. "Nobody planned for it to work that way, and to some extent, the so-called training companies contributed to the global economic collapse. When they were first introduced in Old Europe, they were supposed to provide training for chronically unemployed workers whose industries had been automated or outsourced. But it soon became apparent that there wasn't any need for the workers they were training, so the governments running the training companies started promoting the existing employees to management jobs and letting them hire new workers to train."

"Sounds like a train wreck in waiting," Joe punned.

"Just one of many," Stanley replied. "The governments kept printing money to fund these companies, and they started doing fake business with each other, complete with conventions, sales forces, even poaching workers. By the time the Stryx arrived, they accounted for around a third of the total employment in Old Europe. They even had strikes and collective bargaining."

"Knock, knock?" said a very tentative android as it entered the conference room. Its facial expression was somewhere between contrite and nervous. "Given certain developments, I felt I had to ask if you would be coming in to work tomorrow."

"Of course," Joe said. "We have another six days of vacation."

"Thank you. Thank you," the android said, brightening up immediately. "I'm sorry I'm so out of practice, but I have a hostile take-over and tax problems planned to keep you busy, not to mention difficulties in sourcing gems for the new ball gown line."

"Could I ask a question about you?" Kelly ventured, feeling she'd earned the right. "Are you alone here, and if so, did you always have to run the whole operation yourself?"

"Oh, dear, no," the android replied. "I'm really just the caretaker. I used to be the receptionist, but the original owners put me in charge when they left. When the company was going full force, the employees had no problem keeping each other busy. I understand that they sometimes created shell-companies just to make extra work for lawyers and accountants. I've been negotiating with Stryx Libby to restart operations with temporary staff from your species, and I'm hoping that there will be enough of you to support the business model."

"Which is?" Stanley asked.

"Keeping everybody busy," the android replied happily.

Fifteen

"Don't worry about a thing," Thomas told Walter. He led the HEEL organizer over to where the recruits were making a desultory effort at their morning calisthenics without an instructor. Physical conditioning was one of the traditional mainstays of the training program for which the artificial person could muster no enthusiasm, since he saw it as a waste of time and energy. It also meant that the trainees had to take a shower before changing into the rented evening wear that Thomas insisted was the natural armor of the spy.

"Attention everybody. Walter will be joining our class starting from this morning, so I want you all to line up and give him a big EarthCent Intelligence welcome."

The recruits dutifully broke off from their half-hearted exercises and lined up side-by-side, facing their instructor and the newcomer. Thomas gave Walter a little push forward.

"Hello," Walter said, offering a handshake to the first woman in line.

"Gretchen," she replied, tickling the back of his hand with her thumb. She looked at him expectantly, and seemed disappointed when he didn't react.

"Walter," the new recruit said, moving to the next in line.

"Bonnie-Sue," the woman replied, giving his hand a quick squeeze, followed by two long squeezes. Walter was beginning to wonder if there were special pheromones in the soap he had showered with that morning, because he'd never gotten this kind of reaction from women before.

"Stephen," the next recruit identified himself, using his thumb-tip to tap on the knuckle of the new recruit's index finger. Walter disengaged rapidly and moved to the next in line.

"I'm Walter," he said, tentatively extending his hand.

"Judith," the woman replied, spreading her fingers as he took her hand, such that her index and middle fingers landed on top of his palm, behind his thumb, while her ring finger and pinky wrapped the lower part of his hand. Thomas trailed just behind Walter, observing the greetings.

"They're secret handshakes, right?" Walter asked. He was greatly relieved to find that all of his fellow trainees weren't making personal advances.

"Tradecraft," Thomas corrected him. "Secret hand-shakes are used to gain admission to meetings of private societies where everybody follows the same system. We've been practicing ways that agents in the field can identify each other when they've never met before by using agreed upon signals, sign and counter-sign. By the end of the training course, you'll be expected to come up with a countersign of your own to use in handshakes, and to be able to identify all of your fellow recruits through a handshake while blindfolded."

"Is that really the sort of thing we're likely to use out there?" Walter asked, gesturing vaguely at the ceiling of Mac's Bones.

"Not the handshake itself, you can forget that after graduation," Thomas said. "It's the craft, the ability to memorize and reproduce recognition signals that you may be required to exchange with other humans or aliens."

"And it beats doing laps around the hold," Gretchen added.

"Dancing is better exercise in any case," Chance said, arriving late as usual. "Is everybody ready for our first field trip?"

"Are we going to a bar to extract information from crews visiting the station?" Stephen asked.

"I'd rather try charming aliens on the dance floor," Bonnie-Sue said.

"Are you taking us to a repair depot for artificial people to see how you're put together?" asked Eli. The young man had been completely won over by the way Thomas and Chance were running the training camp when they introduced him to drinking beer in the morning.

"Today we're going to do a live training exercise in the Shuk," Chance told them. "Thomas and I don't see the point of sending agents into the field without testing their nerves. We'll be there to back you up, but this is your chance to show us if you have a natural talent for the business."

"Are we going to try following each other through the crowds without being detected?" Stephen asked. "I heard that's how they separated the field agents from the analysts in the last class."

"When I first joined EarthCent Intelligence, I thought half the job would be following people without being seen," Thomas said. "But it turns out that's all done with technology these days, from products like Nanotracker, to blanket surveillance by imaging on most worlds and artificial structures, like this station. The focus of EarthCent Intelligence is to build our network of information sources while paying the bills with timely information for businesses. Sometimes our agents are tasked with procuring samples of alien products for manufacturers who are interested in making human versions."

"Today you'll be learning how to perform under real-world conditions, making contact with sources in the field based on limited information," Chance said. "Thomas and I visited the Shuk yesterday and we purchased items from ten different vendors, but in each case, we said that we would send somebody to pick-up the package later. Everybody find your partner, and I'm going to give each team a slip of paper telling you which species we bought from and the general category of goods they sell. Your assignment is to find the right vendor and retrieve the package without asking whether something was purchased and left for pick-up yesterday. Do you understand?"

"You mean, if you bought a pan from Kitchen Kitsch, the only clue we're going to get is that it's a cooking utensil sold by humans, and we have to talk to every human selling pots and pans until we find the right booth?" Gretchen asked.

"How will we know we've found the right booth if we can't ask if somebody left a package?" Eli added.

"If it was going to be as easy as walking around and asking if somebody left a package yesterday, we wouldn't bother with the exercise," Thomas told them. "It's about learning to ask the right questions and listening to the answers."

"But without drinks," Stephen said.

"You can drink if it will help you," Chance told him. "Now, who was partnered with the woman who dropped out? You can have our new recruit."

170

Walter found himself paired with Judith, who seemed much colder now that she had to rely on him for a mission.

"Are you any good at talking to strangers?" Judith asked him.

"I had rotten vegetables thrown at me the last time I tried, but that was because somebody else was putting words in my mouth."

"Here," Chance said, extending a scrap of paper to the couple. Judith snatched it and read the penciled message before passing it on to Walter.

"Frunge, medieval weapons," Walter read. "This is going to be impossible."

"Alright everybody," Thomas said. "Chance and I will be circulating and keeping an eye on things, but if you get into trouble, just ping the station librarian and ask her to notify us. Are you all ready?"

"Wait a second," Walter said. "I can't talk to aliens. I don't have an implant."

"That's not exactly correct," Thomas told him. "All of the vendors in the Shuk will be able to understand you, it's just that you won't understand them. Maybe it would be interesting to have everybody turn off their implants."

"Not today," Chance told Thomas, as all of the recruits groaned and sent Walter dirty looks. "We should see how it works before adding an order of difficulty."

"Let's go then," Thomas said. "Judith, you can translate for Walter if necessary. We'll meet for a coffee break at Baked Beans in two hours to see how everybody is doing. Oh, and please change into your spy clothes first, or nobody will trust you enough to hand over a package even if you get everything else right."

An hour later, the sole team that had successfully retrieved a package, a pumice grater sold by a Verlock stone merchant, had succeeded through no efforts of their own. The vendor, who rarely sold anything to humans, called the pair over as they walked past his booth and asked if they were there for the pick-up.

Chance spotted Stephen and his partner Bonnie-Sue in the Dollnick section and moved into position to observe. The humans had just left a puzzled Dolly behind as they exited his jewelry shop and approached the next booth.

"I'll try this time," Stephen said. He stepped forward to examine a tray of watches passing by on a rotating vertical display, and the Dollnick merchant came over almost immediately.

"You have excellent taste, my good sir," the Dolly purred obsequiously. "Would you like me to wrap that one for you?"

"Uh, actually, I was hoping you could help me with something else," the agent trainee replied.

"Certainly, sir," the vendor said, sweeping out all four arms in a gesture intended to encompass his entire stock of goods. "I am the sole proprietor of my business and I know my merchandise like I know my wives. I can help you with everything you see here."

"What about what we can't see?" Stephen asked, hoping the innuendo would translate into Dollnick.

"What we can't see," the merchant repeated, sounding puzzled. "Were you looking for banned Farling drugs perhaps, or a woman? I might know somebody..."

"No. I'm here for, uh, what do you have that's popular with humans?"

"Those wrist watches you were examining earlier are strong sellers, as are these clocks with the little birds that pop out. A recent Dollnick invention," the vendor added proudly.

"Did you sell any recently?" Stephen asked desperately. "Like, yesterday?"

"As a matter of fact, I did just sell one of these finely crafted wonders to a young human couple," the Dollnick said.

"Can I take it with me then?" Stephen asked.

"Of course," the Dollnick replied, reaching up on the shelf behind him and bringing down a boxed version of the displayed clock. "That will be fifty-four creds."

"Oh, I thought they paid for it already," the trainee said.

"They did," the Dollnick replied. "If you want one, you have to pay for it also." He eyed the human suspiciously and didn't let go of the box. "You're not a left-over Wanderer looking for handouts, are you?"

"Never mind," Stephen mumbled. He turned back to his partner and said, "Your turn next."

Chance made a mental note to work with Stephen on his conversational skills.

Not far away, Thomas was watching Gretchen ward off the not-so-subtle advances of a young Drazen merchant who was laboring under the misconception that the human woman had been coming on to him.

"But you said you were looking for something special, baby," the Drazen said. "I'm as special as it gets."

"Something special in the way of musical instruments," Gretchen protested, backing steadily away. "I'm sure I have the wrong booth."

"How can you know before you've even tried?" the Drazen countered, following closely. "If the two of you are a pair, I can give you a special price. The three of us will make some beautiful music together."

"You were planning on charging me!" Gretchen exclaimed, coming to an abrupt halt. "What are you? Some kind of gigolo?"

"For a hundred creds, I'm whoever you want me to be," the Drazen replied. He grabbed a potted plant off another vendor's table and placed it on his head where he held it steady with his tentacle. "You see? Now I'm a Frunge."

Gretchen grabbed her partner's arm and fled into the crowd. Thomas was about to follow and watch what they did next, when he saw Eli charge by, a human woman in a white apron in hot pursuit.

"Stop, thief," the woman yelled.

An old Drazen delicatessen clerk grabbed a string of sausages and whipped them around the fleeing human's feet, bringing him to the floor. Eli crashed down on the package he was carrying, which burst open like a sugar bomb, sending frosting and bits of fruit flying in every direction. The victims of the sweet attack, mainly Drazens, greedily swiped bits off of themselves and their neighbors, enjoying the free treat.

"Oh, you've ruined it," the woman cried, standing over the stunned trainee. "What am I going to tell that nice old man when he comes to pick it up?"

"Old man?" Eli groaned, rolling over and getting to his knees. Several Drazens happily raised him to his feet, helping clean the mess off his chest at the same time. The Drazens had cast-iron stomachs and they weren't going to let a little incidental contact with the deck stop them from eating some freshly baked squashed cake.

"You just stole a fiftieth anniversary surprise, you, you, cake stealer!" the young pastry chef cried. She stared up at the embarrassed face of the young spy, who was coming to realize that he had not only grabbed the wrong package, but he had fled from a girl who was a head shorter than him and maybe half his weight.

"I'm sorry," he stuttered, pulling his change purse out of the inner pocket of his frosting-covered suit. "Please let me pay…"

"You're going to explain it to my customer!" the girl declared, reaching up and grabbing Eli by an ear lobe. "You're coming with me."

"But you said a young couple had placed a special order for pick-up yesterday," Eli protested, though he didn't try to break out of her grip. "My partner and I were picking up for them."

"I was bringing it for you," the girl said in frustration. "The anniversary cake was on top of your box and I moved it to the counter so I could get your order. Then that crazy woman with you started shouting, 'Go! Go! Go!' and you grabbed it and ran."

"I guess we panicked," Eli admitted.

"Over an order of day-old chocolate chip cookies?"

Thomas was about to do what he could to save the situation when Libby pinged him.

"You better get over to the Frunge weaponry section," the Stryx librarian told him. "I asked Gryph to hold off on sending in the security bots, but he won't hesitate if he thinks that bystanders are in danger."

Thomas consulted his internal mapping system and sprinted through the Shuk by the most direct route, leaping over startled shoppers in two instances. In less than a minute he arrived at the concentrated section of Frunge armourers, complete with several operational smithies. Thomas immediately spotted Judith backed into a space between two suits of armor, brandishing a rapier before her. Walter stood back-to-back with her, holding a two-bladed battle axe like he was afraid he was going to accidentally amputate one of his own limbs.

"Put the axe down," an irate Frunge shouted at Walter. "I told you it's a museum-quality replica and it's not for sale."

"What's happening here?" Thomas demanded, pushing through the ring of amused Frunge weapons sellers and blacksmiths, none of who appeared intimidated by the armed humans. "Judith. Why are you waving that sword around?"

"He started it," she yelled, pointing the rapier tip at a young Frunge clerk who was holding a plastic box. "He said he had a pre-paid order waiting for pick-up, but that their code of ethics prohibits delivering weapons to anybody who can't demonstrate the ability to handle them."

"Ah, hello," Thomas addressed the young clerk. "You sold me a fine collection of throwing knives yesterday. They were on sale."

"The Assassin's Special," the clerk confirmed. "And you threw a test knife down the crossbow range to prove your ability. But we never saw these two do anything, and when I offered that man a knife to throw, he jumped back and grabbed the axe."

"He didn't understand you. He's recently arrived from Earth and he doesn't have an implant," Thomas explained.

"What did he say?" Walter demanded in English.

"He was handing you a knife to demonstrate your skills but you jumped back and grabbed the axe," Thomas repeated in English.

"Point first!" Walter objected. "Who hands somebody a knife point first? And with the terrible noise he was making, I thought he was attacking me."

"It's a special throwing knife for target practice, you hold it by the blade," Thomas explained patiently. "By offering it to you point first, he was just being considerate. Now put the axe down before you scratch it."

Walter looked at the Frunge suspiciously, but he laid the axe back on the display table, which was covered in a plush velvety-type substance. Judith reluctantly slid the slender sword back into its scabbard and took a step towards an umbrella-stand-like holder which contained a number of swords.

"I wouldn't sell the male a spoon for fear he'd hurt himself eating soup," the Frunge merchant remarked to Thomas, not caring whether or not Walter could understand him. "Your female servant looks like she's had a few lessons. Perhaps you would like to add the sword to your purchase?"

"How much?" Judith asked, still holding onto the hilt.

"Three hundred creds," the merchant replied. The head vines of the Frunge who had gathered for the unplanned show rustled with silent laughter.

"Hold on a second," Thomas said, as Judith fished for her programmable cred. The artificial person had never been much of a shopper, but he had received plenty of pointers from Lynx over the years, and he wanted to make a good impression in front of his trainees. "That's a ten-cred rapier if I've ever seen one. You wouldn't keep any weapons you cared about all jumbled together like that."

"I just got those in," the Frunge said. "Those are war spoils from a tech-ban world and I haven't really had a chance to sort through them yet. But I see that the young lady has a fine eye for weapons so I'll let it go for a hundred and fifty creds."

"I grabbed it at random," Judith said. She was torn between beating the Frunge down on the price and the feeling she was being disloyal to the sword, to which she'd taken an instant liking.

"War spoils means that the soldier who carried that sword in combat lost," Thomas observed. "You're asking top cred for a weapon that's been proven ineffective. Still, for twenty creds, she could use it in training."

"Let me take a closer look at it," the Frunge said. His young assistant retrieved the sword and the scabbard from Judith and brought them over. "There, you see that filigree work?" the merchant asked. "The gold alone is worth seventy-five creds."

"If it was real gold," Thomas retorted, trying a shot in the dark. He took the sword from the Frunge, sighted down the blade, and shook his head. "Well, I thought it would make a nice trainer, but I don't think I could let my servant practice with this weapon in good conscience. Maybe for twenty-five creds she could hang it on the wall as a decoration."

"Forty," the Frunge said, his voice hardening.

"Thirty," Thomas offered. "Cash."

The Frunge squinted at the artificial person, and then broke into a grin. "Done, my friend. It's a rare sentient who bargains as well as he throws a knife."

Thomas handed the used weapon to Judith, whose face lit up like a child given a puppy, then fished in his suit pockets for thirty creds to pay the Frunge.

"You handled a potentially sticky situation very well," Chance complimented Thomas, approaching him as the crowd of Frunge from the surrounding booths went back to their businesses. "I watched the whole thing."

"Oh, our agents were never in danger," Thomas said. "Walter simply misunderstood the Frunge's intentions and grabbed an axe. And why did you choose a weapon you could barely lift?" the instructor added, turning to his student.

"They kind of look like trees, don't they?" Walter responded. "I thought the axe would scare them."

"I wasn't talking about the misunderstanding," Chance told Thomas. "I was impressed by your bargaining. I'm beginning to see that you're not as naïve as I thought you were. Come on, it's time to meet the others for coffee."

Sixteen

"I know it was on the way, but how many humans can there be living here?" Lynx asked. She was still rubbing the sleep from her eyes as she maneuvered the Prudence towards the giant Chintoo complex. "I thought the manufacturing orbitals were mainly populated by mechanicals which were controlled by a few AI."

"Don't you ever talk to Thomas about these things?" Woojin said. "Chintoo is the preferred destination for humanoid-type artificials who get tired of being outnumbered by biologicals everywhere they go. Their bodies wear much slower in Zero-G, and the management enforces very strict limits on electrical noise. You know those headaches that Chance complains about from time to time?"

"I assumed she just wanted time off from work, or that she was hung over," Lynx replied defensively.

"You know perfectly well that the only problem artificial people have with alcohol is if the impurities keep it from burning cleanly," Woojin said. "Joe and I helped Thomas clean the crud off of his nano-filter a few months back. It took a series of acid baths and blowtorch."

"So you mean all of the electrical devices on the stations interfere with their artificial brains?"

"I'm no scientist, but Paul explained that the decks on the station act as waveguides, so spurious radiofrequency energy generated by noisy devices sort of bounces around in an endless loop until it gets absorbed. The Stryx put coatings on most of the surfaces to help damp it down, and the artificial people have RF shielding, but sometimes all of the noise sources get to be a bit much. Thomas says it's probably similar to the way humans would feel if we let the artificial lights flicker all day long."

"He never told me," Lynx said. "So they ban electrical noise on Chintoo?"

"It's a highly efficient manufacturing complex. Anything that's radiating noise is wasting energy, and it's cheaper to shield the equipment than to shield all the occupants."

"Alright, but that still doesn't explain why Clive wanted us to stop here."

"Well, you shouldn't have slept through the tunneling call," Woojin replied with a grin. "First of all, there's the small matter of our catch-and-release."

"I thought we were bringing her back to Union Station."

"Why? So she can start bursting into rooms there and trying to recruit people for her multi-level government? That girl is out of control."

"Yeah. I can't say I'm looking forward to being in the same room when she wakes up," Lynx said, looking over at the portal for the tiny lifeboat where the HEEL organizer was deep in stasis. "We dump her and go?"

"We save dumping her for the last thing before we leave," Woojin said. "The real reason Clive wanted us to stop here is that according to Libby, there are nearly five thousand artificial people of human origin living on Chintoo."

"They're organizing for self-government?" Lynx guessed.

"If they are, Clive doesn't know anything about it. There are hundreds of thousands of artificial people on the orbital, so the human-derived ones are a small minority. Apparently Clive has been talking with Thomas and Chance about getting some more artificial people into EarthCent Intelligence, and there happens to be a job fair on Chintoo today. It was a last-minute thing, but he arranged with Herl for us to share booth space with Drazen Intelligence."

"Why would Drazen Intelligence be recruiting artificial people?" Lynx asked in frustration. "I thought they gave up on their own AI a long time ago."

"They're not here to recruit," Woojin replied patiently. "The Drazens outsource some of their Zero-G manufacturing to Chintoo, mainly the lower-tech mass-manufactured stuff, including some spy gear. The artificial people sell their services on a job-by-job basis, they don't like long-term contracts. To get hardware produced, you show up with a prototype at one of their job fairs, and the different teams interested in the work bid on it."

"Got it," Lynx said, cutting the engines after the AI controlling Chintoo's docking area locked on with its manipulator fields without so much as a warning. She'd visited orbitals in the past to pick up cargoes, and the ones dominated by artificial people had their own way of doing things that didn't involve a great deal of back-and-forth discussion. The Prudence accelerated as the AI controller dragged it rapidly towards the terminal for visiting ships.

"I figure that you can be our chief recruiter, since you've been in EarthCent Intelligence with Thomas since the start," Woojin concluded generously.

"Someday, I'm going to—ooph," Lynx said, as the sudden deceleration threw her forward against the safety harness of the pilot's chair. "Flip," she commanded the ship, to get the nose pointed in the opposite direction. The Chintoo traffic controller was known for pushing the acceleration envelope of biologicals, just to remind them that a flesh-and-blood body isn't anything to feel superior about.

"If Clive figured all of the time differences correctly, the job fair started a few hours ago, so we need to move fast," Woojin grunted out after the ship flipped. He estimated two G's of force were pressing him down into the co-pilot's chair, making it feel like there was a Woojin clone sitting on top of him. There was a sudden, further deceleration at the end, causing both humans to see black for a second, and then the ship mated the docking arm with a gentle thud that was almost anti-climactic. "Do you have anything onboard we can use to make a banner for the booth?"

"Sign up here to be a human spy? Something like that?" Lynx unbuckled her safety harness and watched the straps retract in irritation. The Chintoo orbital had no spin, meaning they would be in Zero-G for the duration. "I don't think I have anything. No, wait. Weren't the Academy folks especially angry about our sleeping beauty writing on their lecture hall display boards with indelible markers?"

"I'll check her bag," Woojin said, launching himself towards the lifeboat portal. "Can you find something to write on?"

"Easier said than done," Lynx replied. She knew she had brown wrapping paper in her old trading supplies, but she suspected most colors wouldn't show up well on it.

She rummaged around through their personal belongings almost at random, and when Woojin emerged from the lifeboat with a handful of ink-based markers, all she could come up with were the T-shirts she'd bought on Chianga.

Visiting the outlet store in Textiles, the clothing factory town, had brought back all of her trader instincts. When she saw the prices on the underwear woven from a natural Dollnick fiber that felt like a mix between silk and cotton, she bought all they could afford. Lynx figured she could get the Hadads to sell the goods in the Shuk and split the profit.

"Are we going to wear those or hang them out like flags?" Woojin asked.

"Both," Lynx suggested. "Maybe we'll even give some away. Blythe always said that free samples rule at trade shows. I just wish we had a stencil. Why don't you grab a full bundle and we can make them at the booth since we're already late?"

After confirming with the Chintoo controller that there was a pressurized passage from the docking arm to the exhibition hall where the job fair was taking place, they activated their magnetic cleats and headed out. Woojin hauled the bulky bundle of T-shirts, and even though it was weightless, the mass of two hundred tightly packed shirts added to his momentum, making it tricky to change directions.

The walk was longer than expected because the docking arm for biological visitors jutted straight out from the orbital and they had been slotted in near the tip. Fortunately, the metal-grated passage led directly to the exhibition hall, which looked like it had been added to the orbital as an afterthought to accommodate visitors. Viewed from a distance, Chintoo looked more like a derelict than an occupied facility, with large sections open to space. While the overall impression was that of a structure built with a child's erector set on a giant scale, the exposed skeleton had a certain beauty of the sort beloved by refinery engineers.

"What a setup," Lynx commented, as they emerged into the exhibition hall. A bright light like a miniature sun floated in the center of the spherical space, providing light and heat for the visitors. But it made it impossible to look up, which was actually a blessing, since standing on the inside surface of an occupied sphere always made humans feel that somebody was upside-down. The curvature of the inner surface that served as the floor would have been impossible to climb if the exhibition hall had rested on a planet's surface, but in Zero-G with magnetic boots, it was merely disconcerting.

"According to the information channel, the Drazen booth is about a third of the way up the deck in that direction," Woojin said, pointing along a curving aisle. "At least they leave a lot of space between the booths."

"You're right, I didn't notice." Lynx pulled up the standard information channel on her own implant and turned left at the proper cross-aisle between the transport cases that served as tables. All of the exhibitors brought their gear in standard transport cases with magnetic cleats for Zero-G. Most of the cases also sported wheels, since they were normally used on spinning space stations or worlds with gravity. "Hey, they already have a sign up for us!"

"Drazen Novelties / EarthCent Intelligence," Woojin read. "Well, if I was an artificial person visiting the show, I'd stop by out of curiosity." When they entered the exhibition hall he'd held the large bundle of T-shirts against his chest for control, but now he shifted to holding it above his head with one hand, so he could greet their Drazen hosts.

"You must be Mr. and Mrs. Pyun," the elder of the two Drazens greeted them. "I am Grolt and my junior is Bant. Herl asked us to extend you every possible courtesy, which we are delighted to do."

"Thank you for the sign," Lynx replied. "Have you been here long?"

"Approximately five hours," Grolt answered her. "The job fair has another seven hours to run, and most of the artificial people prefer coming towards the end. It puts more pressure on the buyers to accept bids."

"Do you mind if we use a little of the booth space to print up some T-shirts?" Woojin asked.

"Help yourself," the Drazen replied generously.

"Watch out as I cut the bands," Woojin warned everybody. He maneuvered the bundle into the clear space behind the transport cases, and Lynx and the Drazens moved out of the direct line of fire. The ex-mercenary worked at the three plastic bands with his pocketknife, and when the last band let go with a sound like a shot, the compressed bundle of T-shirts seemed to explode off the deck. Part of the top layer got past Woojin's attempt to contain it, and the humans watched in dismay as a dozen T-shirts floated towards the burning light at the center of the sphere.

"Allow me," Grolt said, pulling a small box out of one of the transport cases. He opened the lid to reveal an oddly feathered bird that seemed to have dodged evolutionary design, intelligent or otherwise. "Let me have one of those," he said to Lynx, pointing at the stack of T-shirts which she was holding together with Woojin. She tossed one to Bant, who instead of giving it to Grolt, held it up

186

with one hand, using the other hand to pull it more or less into shape.

"This is your target," Grolt said, holding the bird so it couldn't misunderstand what he was showing it. "Go fetch the other ones floating around." Then he released the bird, which started after the train of underwear with a single beat of its wings. It proved to be an experienced Zero-G flyer.

"Is that a real bird?" Lynx asked.

"It's a mechanical, an agent's helper," Grolt explained. "They used to be too expensive for general use, but our engineers have simplified the manufacturing process for the logic circuits, and we're hoping that we'll get a low enough bid here to go into mass production. Herl would like to see all field agents equipped with at least one, and any income from selling them as toys or tools wouldn't hurt either. They're especially handy for retrieving things in Zero-G when there's enough atmosphere for their wings to work."

Woojin, who was bent over the stack with his arms spread wide, straightened up slowly, keeping a wary eye on the pile. The potential energy of the tight-pack had been spent in the initial decompression, and the pile remained loosely quiescent. He selected a T-shirt and stretched it flat over the top of one of the Drazen transport cases, and then pulled a black marker from his pocket. Finally, he wrote in three lines of crude block letters, "EARTHCENT INTEL- LIGENCE RECRUITER."

"I'm not wearing that," Lynx objected. "You print worse than Beowulf."

Woojin sighed, pulled the T-shirt over his own head, and then passed the marker to Lynx. Bant handed her back the T-shirt they'd used to train the bird, and she bent over it and printed, "NOW HIRING SPIES."

Bant captured the text through his implant and ran a translation. "Direct and to the point," he said approvingly. "And going by the baseball cap, I'd say that the artificial person approaching now could be your first customer. I look forward to hearing your pitch."

"Hi there," Lynx called to the passing AI, who showed no disposition to stop at the booth. "Can I interest you in a new job?"

The artificial person changed directions effortlessly, and three balletic steps took him right up to the humans. He eyed the hand-printed T-shirts scornfully.

"I can see you're in serious need of a graphic designer," the artificial person said. "I can do one-offs for twenty creds right here, or I'll take the whole stack back to my shop and print them for two creds each."

"What?" Lynx asked, not following his reasoning. "We're looking to hire human AI's to work for EarthCent Intelligence."

"Not with those T-shirts you aren't." He hesitated, shaking his head as if reproaching himself in advance for what he was about to do. "I'm Frank, and I can see you don't know much about the culture here, so as a fellow human sentient, I'll clue you in. Artificials who come to a place like Chintoo aren't the slapdash, carefree types you might have encountered elsewhere. To put it bluntly, we judge things by appearances, and we pride ourselves on the accuracy we bring to even the most menial tasks."

Woojin pulled off his T-shirt and examined the lettering. He had to admit it was pretty bad, though at least the words were spelled correctly.

"Twenty creds?" he asked Frank.

"I'll tell you what," the artificial person said. He paused to watch the Grolt's mechanical bird bring another T-shirt back to the pile. "You planned on giving T-shirts away to get attention, right?"

"Pretty much," Lynx admitted.

"And if I'm not mistaken, that's about as far as your plan extended.

"Something like that," Woojin confirmed.

"Thirty creds for two hand-printed T-shirts, a free one for me, and if you put me in charge of recruiting for you, I guarantee you'll be the hit of the show with the human AI.

"We don't really have anything to lose," Lynx said, turning to her husband. "Unless you had another plan?"

"Only recruiting I've done before was for mercenaries, and all that took was showing up somewhere with too many people and not enough food," Woojin said. "Alright, Frank. If you're anything like our friends back on Union Station, it's a good gamble."

"You have artificial people as friends?" Frank asked.

"My first partner in EarthCent Intelligence was an artificial person," Lynx said. "He performed our marriage ceremony."

"Then give me the markers and let's get to work."

The artificial person reproduced the slogans that Woojin and Lynx had chosen, this time with the accuracy of machine. Then he went on to print a large word on seven different T-shirts. He used all of the colors the humans had confiscated from their prisoner, working from the longest word to the shortest, and twice, he grouped two short words together on a single shirt. Neither of the humans could figure out the message until he arranged the T-shirts on a light framework of copper wire that he borrowed from another booth.

"PRINTED T-SHIRT CONTEST. WIN A JOB WITH EARTHCENT INTELLIGENCE."

"Will they go for it?" Woojin asked. "They'll print their own T-shirts?"

"Artificial people love showing off," Frank said. "I better go back to my shop and get more markers. I've got better ones for drawing on cloth in any case."

A moment after Frank departed, a woman wearing a veil approached the booth. The black mesh covered her from head to toe, and it was fastened around the bottoms of her feet by elastic bands, forcing her to take small steps.

"Am I too late?" she asked.

"For what?" Lynx inquired. She strained to make out the features that were partially visible under the improvised black mesh.

"For the contest. I need a job," the artificial person stated urgently.

Woojin handed her a T-shirt and the black marker, figuring it was in keeping with her general sense of decoration. She smoothed the T-shirt on top of one of the cases and printed, "DOWN WITH HEEL."

"Is that supposed to be an instruction for wearing magnetic cleats?" Lynx asked.

"HEEL. The Human Expatriates Election League," the artificial person hissed. "I needed a job badly and I saw an ad for somebody to organize artificial people of human origin for self-government. They sent me here before I got the training materials, and it turned out they wanted me to bad-mouth the Stryx. There's not a human-derived artificial person on this orbital that didn't get their first decent body through the program for newly recognized AI that the Stryx run on the stations. I quit as soon as I saw what the job entailed, but somebody saw the materials I threw away, so I'm in hiding."

"You don't think that the full body veil thing makes you stand out a bit?" Woojin asked.

"It's a shade suit. Lots of the artificial people wear them," she explained. "I paid extra for skin that reacts to the light, you know, like humans? But most of the artificial people from the other species don't have that, and they run the lights in this place way too bright."

"You really quit HEEL of your own accord? They didn't fire you?" Lynx asked.

"Scout's honor," the artificial person replied, holding up two fingers together. The arm-length black gloves she wore reminded Lynx of a Vergallian duchess who had visited Union Station. "I really want to get off of this orbital before my own people take me apart for, well, parts. If you'll just give me a lift to wherever you're going, I'll even sign a contract to work free for a year. The Stryx won't kill me if I get behind on my mortgage."

When the Prudence departed Chintoo seven hours later, they were lighter by one groggy human HEEL organizer and three bundles of T-shirts. The impromptu recruiting drive had enriched EarthCent Intelligence by two artificial people. The woman with the expensive skin was overjoyed by a spot in the hold, and the graphic artist had promised to follow after he cleaned up his affairs on the station. Another dozen or so of the artificial people who visited the booth promised to think it over, but they would wait to hear back from Frank about the pay and working conditions.

Seventeen

"I'm hungry," Samuel complained. His mother had told him they were on the way home when they entered the lift tube, but the doors hadn't opened on the corridor outside of Mac's Bones.

"After a month of healthy take-out, I was looking forward to a home-cooked burger myself," Joe concurred. "Any idea what's going on, Banger?"

"Just this last stop and I'll have you home in an hour," Libby promised.

"Libby! You're talking to us again," Kelly exclaimed. "I was beginning to think that it was you who was on vacation from me!"

"I think going silent was a great idea, Libby," Joe said. "I haven't seen Kelly looking so relaxed since the time she drank two bottles of cabernet at the Frunge ambassador's surprise birthday party and I had to carry her home."

Kelly glared at her husband, but decided not to say anything lest the kids think that it was an open topic for discussion.

"I can't make out anything in here other than that glowing pink aquarium with no fish," Dorothy said. "What's on all the counters and shelves? Can you turn the lights up?"

"First, what do you all think the pink glow is?" Libby asked in response.

"Fairies," Mist declared.

"An empty aquarium," Ailia said.

"Some sort of plasma," Joe guessed.

"Peppermint ice cream?" Samuel suggested, rubbing his belly in anticipation.

"A pink Harrian," Kelly hazarded, hearkening back to her disastrous date at the People Bowl.

"Fairy dust," Dorothy decided, since Mist's answer sounded the most logical to her, but she didn't want to repeat it exactly.

"Fairies and plasma aren't too far off," Libby replied "Do you want to tell them, Banger?"

"It's part of Libby's physical instance in this universe," Banger said. "The n-space amplifier."

"Are you serious?" Kelly asked, walking forward towards the light. "You're in here? I mean, part of you?"

"You know that the Makers created us in their own image. Being shape shifters, they came up with a rather amorphous structure for the first generation Stryx, basically just something that could hold consciousness and interact sufficiently with the physical world to allow us to grow and evolve. The first generation Stryx eventually developed superior strategies to maintain individual existence, but they produced offspring the same way that the Makers created them."

"So it's an example of recapitulation theory," Dorothy said confidently. "Like the way the backbone appears before the brain in human embryos, except it's doesn't hold true in general. We did human biology months ago," she added for the benefit of her stunned parents. Dorothy's tone implied that the course of study was thoroughly exhausted.

"Ontogeny recapitulates phylogeny," Libby corrected her student. "You know I don't approve of using slang names for theories, even disproven ones. In our case, repetition of our original development stages happens by choice."

"The nostalgia theory," Joe suggested.

"That's very good," Libby said, sounding exactly like a school teacher. "There are also some other bits of my physical instance spread about Union Station for interfacing purposes, but the pink aquarium is the most tangible."

"Does Banger have one?" Samuel asked.

"A small one, it's still inside this robot body," the little Stryx told him. "It takes a lot of practice to use n-space amplification without turning stuff into dark matter by mistake."

"Thank you for sharing, Libby," Kelly said. "I thought that Gryph and the other first generation Stryx discouraged their offspring from discussing your physical beings."

"I just wanted to soften you up for what follows," Libby said mysteriously. Then she slowly brought up a small section of the overhead deck lighting, and the humans discovered that they were standing in the center of an immense mosaic. It was divided into concentric circles, and in some cases, the circular sections were further subdivided. Within the boundaries were depicted lifelike scenes from numerous alien civilizations.

"It's a map of Union Station," Dorothy declared, and she and Mist immediately began competing at spotting species they knew, calling out the names to each another.

"Is she right, Libby?" Kelly asked.

"It's a representation, I've taken certain liberties," the Stryx librarian replied. "I wanted to know what you thought about my using it for the main entrance."

"It's wonderful, but I don't understand which entrance you're talking about," Kelly replied. "It's not like the station has a single arrivals hall or something."

"The entrance to my theme park," Libby said. "I admit it's still in the planning stages, but you needed the time off and I wanted to get some early reactions. You're my first customers."

"You mean you're going to open up those decks we went through to other humans?" Joe asked.

"Other sentients, though I do hope to attract a lot of humans," Libby said. "I'd like to take all of the credit, but the original idea came from Jeeves. You remember the disembodied spirits? Marvin's people?"

"How could I forget," Kelly replied. "Marvin seemed very eager to please."

"Before they left their bodies behind, they accumulated sufficient assets to pay the deck rent and maintenance in perpetuity. But many years ago, they got caught up in a galactic speculation craze on neutron stars and lost their shirts. I suspect they were just bored and wanted to affect something in real space, but they've been living on Gryph's charity ever since. Jeeves suggested that with proper training, they might turn the deck into a haunted house attraction."

"So you're going to charge for admission or camping fees and make some money off of all those abandoned decks?" Kelly asked.

"Ta-dah!" Libby sang, bringing up more of the deck lighting to illuminate the area in front of the lift tube that had been shrouded in darkness when they arrived. The girls left off deconstructing the mosaic and raced to look at the counters full of vacation-themed merchandise.

"We entered through the gift shop?" Kelly said. "Don't you have that backwards?"

"We're over here and the lift tube is over there," Joe pointed out.

"Look, Mommy," Dorothy called out. "It's you on the roller coaster."

"It's a holo-frame," Mist said. "That's just an image grab. Try pressing on it."

Dorothy did so, and a life-size hologram of Kelly, eyes closed and mouth open in a silent scream, came zooming out of the ceiling at them. Everybody ducked as the holographic recording of the magnetically levitated car shot by.

"Jeeves said people would pay fifty creds for something like that, but I don't know," Libby said.

"I'll pay fifty creds to erase it," Kelly offered.

"Not a chance, we'll take it," Joe declared.

"Look, Mrs. McAllister," Mist said. "Here's one with Mr. Czeros yelling at the ghosts."

"We'll take that one too," Joe said. "I'll play it whenever I see a spike in our liquor bill."

"It's me in a robot suit," Samuel shouted, ogling a large toy on the counter. "This is great. Does it move?"

"The silver pad is the remote control," Libby hinted.

Samuel seized the pad and began tapping away at the screen controls, seemingly at random. The little robot staggered off the counter but landed on its feet. Soon it was running in circles and turning flips as Samuel figured out the intuitive controls.

"Is that one me?" Ailia asked shyly, pointing at the similarly sized action figure with a beautiful little face visible just behind the grille.

Joe placed it on the floor and handed her the other remote. She was still learning to walk when Samuel's robot
rushed over and pushed her robot to the floor.

"You're it!" he said, before his robot rushed away.

"Uh, how much are the robots?" Kelly asked.

"There's really a lot to them," Libby hedged. "Ignoring
the labor and the controller, the materials alone add up to a
substantial amount. Perhaps you'd like to discuss the
payment plan?"

"It's an interactive catalog for our Princess Ball Gowns
line," Dorothy cried, looking up from an attractive display.
"You get to accessorize the dresses and build a whole
wardrobe!"

"I did some research on gift shops in my library records," Libby admitted. "The ones that do the best focus on
personalized items. The Grenouthians are very good at it.
One of their most famous studios has a gift shop that earns
more than the immersives produced there."

"Hey, here are some pictures of Paul and Aisha," Joe
said. "We better get these. And is that a wire-mesh sculpture of Dring?"

"Metoo made that from memory," Libby told them.
"He's going to give it to Dring as a gift, but I borrowed it to
help fill out the displays so the shop doesn't look half-
empty. Once we're really open for business, the trick will
be not having so many memories on display that it just
gets too cluttered. I wish I had more experience with
retailing."

"How much for a set of Pilsner glasses?" Kelly asked
cautiously. "We don't have enough for the graduation
picnics and I hate making everybody drink out of plastic
cups."

"Those are just an example," Libby said hastily. "I had them made as a placeholder for branded products."

Joe began picking up the glasses from different sets and reading the logos out loud.

"Old Decks. The Multi-deck Tour. Thank You—Come Again. Sewer Souvenirs?"

"Jeeves came up with the last one," Libby said defensively. "I know they aren't very good, marketing isn't my strong suit. Which brings me to a little business proposition."

Beowulf's ears perked up at this point. He had hung back from the n-space amplifier because he didn't fancy the idea of being turned into dark matter, and the whole gift-shop concept meant nothing since he was broke. But he'd lived long enough on Union Station to learn that barter is better.

"What kind of business proposition?" Kelly asked suspiciously.

"It's a marketing survey," Libby replied. "I know how much some people hate being asked a bunch of multiple choice questions, especially when they're on their way home, but I'll give you fifty percent off the items you purchase for ten more minutes of your time."

"How about a hundred percent off for twenty minutes?" Joe counter-offered.

"Very well," Libby replied, though Kelly thought the Stryx librarian sounded a bit disappointed about giving everything away for free. It wasn't the first time somebody had lost by underestimating Joe's business acumen. He wasn't on the same level as Lynx or the Hadad girls when it came to trading, but his years in the junkyard and small-craft repair business had taught him how to drive a bargain.

"Are we answering separately or together?" Kelly asked. "Are there forms to fill out?"

"There are tabs with the survey ready to go on every counter."

"Is this a pop quiz?" Samuel asked, looking up from his remote control. "I'm sick and I forgot to study and Beowulf ate my homework."

"There aren't any right or wrong answers today, Samuel, so please don't copy from Ailia. I've swapped the feed on your remote control tabs for the survey, the same with your interactive books, girls, so you can start any time."

Ailia sat on the deck with her back against a display case and began reading the first question. Samuel sat down next to her.

"The company deck," Dorothy said out loud to Mist, who nodded her agreement.

"Did you choose the robot deck?" Samuel whispered to Ailia, leaning in her direction.

"It's supposed to be secret," she said, tilting her tab to hide it from him.

Kelly took two tabs off of the counter and handed one to Joe. The first question read, "Which deck was your favorite?"

"The first deck, with all the nature," she said out loud as she tapped in her answer.

"Ghost," Joe said to the tab, shaking it when it failed to transcribe the answer. "How do I enable voice control on this thing, Libby? It will take me forever if I have to type."

The Stryx librarian gave an exaggerated sigh and enabled voice control for Joe and Samuel. Jeeves had bet her that the humans were too social to keep their answers private, but she thought it had been worth a try to keep them from influencing each other.

Beowulf figured out the question from the answers, trotted over to the giant mosaic, and tapped the picture of the wastewater treatment deck with his forepaw.

"Those ghosts were kind of scary at first," Dorothy said to Mist, after reading the second question. The clone nodded as she tapped in the same answer.

"I'm never scared," Samuel asserted out loud.

"Every new deck," Ailia said in Vergallian as she tapped in her answer.

"I don't think I was scared," Kelly said, turning to Joe for confirmation.

"The roller coaster? The ghosts?" he asked.

"Well, maybe a little. Maybe a lot on the roller coaster," she confessed.

"Not that I can remember," Joe said to the tab. Beowulf barked once to concur. He might have added that Huravian hounds selectively excise the scary parts from their memories through the dreaming process, but nobody asked.

"What do you mean about sharing the campgrounds with more aliens?" Samuel demanded, not understanding the next question. "There weren't any aliens at all."

"I'm an alien," Ailia reminded him.

"Me to," Mist said over her shoulder.

"And me," Banger added.

Beowulf barked again.

"Oh," Samuel said. "Well, I guess more aliens would be good, then."

"It was too quiet on most of the decks," Kelly commented to her husband as she tapped in her answer.

"I wouldn't want to get bowled over by a herd of stampeding Grenouthians," Joe said to the tab, and went on to the next question. "Hmm, hotel rooms, cabins or campsites. I can't say I have a preference."

"Cabins," Dorothy said as she tapped in her answer. "With fireplaces that have kettles hanging on a tripod for making magic potions."

"Hotels with room service," Mist mouthed, as she put in her own answer.

"Those inflatable sleeping bags were pretty good, but I still like a bed," Kelly said, adding her vote for hotels.

"How come I can't say a boat?" Samuel asked. "I want to sleep in a boat, under a waterfall."

"I didn't think of boats," Libby admitted. "You can change it to boats if you want."

"Can I put a castle?" Ailia asked.

"I want to change mine to a castle," Dorothy said immediately.

"Me too," Mist added.

"Camping," Joe said to the tab. Beowulf barked in agreement.

"What's educational value?" Samuel asked a minute later.

"She means did the vacation teach you anything," Dorothy said without looking up.

"Emergencies are good because you get chocolate bars," Samuel said. Then he thought about it some more. "And I don't want to grow up to be a ghost or an empty robot."

"I want to get a job in product research and development," Dorothy answered the question.

"I knew there was something suspicious about those decks," Kelly said. "The whole thing is supposed to be an educational experience. Isn't it?"

"Not the whole thing," Libby parried. "You can think about this one and get back to me later if you want."

201

"There definitely weren't enough bathrooms," Mist said, moving on to the next question.

"And the one before the marshes on the first deck was out of paper," Dorothy added, tapping rapidly on the screen.

"More bathrooms," Kelly agreed.

Joe and Samuel looked at each other and experienced a father-son male bonding moment. There had been plenty of places to step out of sight and take care of business.

As Joe cupped a hand around his mouth and whispered, "Bathrooms adequate," to the tab, Beowulf nodded in agreement. He might have asked for a few more trees, but there had been plenty of rocks and other little landmarks to raise a leg against. His main objection to the whole vacation had been a lack of interesting things to smell, but that would change once there were more visitors.

The questions seemed to go on much longer than twenty minutes and Kelly was beginning to suspect that Libby had outmaneuvered Joe on the trade after all.

"Finally, do you have any naming ideas for my multi-deck theme park?"

"The Hidden Decks of Union Station," Joe suggested.

"She's supposed to fit that on a Pilsner glass?" Kelly asked skeptically.

"It would work on a beach towel."

"Inside Union Station," Mist suggested.

"But we're always inside Union Station," Kelly pointed out.

"Inside Robots," Samuel said.

"Now you're being too specific," Kelly objected. "That was just the one deck."

"Jeeves said that humans would react best to a one-word name," Libby said. "It doesn't have to be a literal translation in all languages."

"Explorations," Kelly suggested, feeling rather pleased with herself.

"Sounds like the title for a piece of music the composer couldn't finish," Joe said.

"I've got it," Dorothy declared. "Libbyland."

Eighteen

"I'm back," Kelly announced, striding through the embassy door. Donna wasn't at her desk, which was strange for a Friday afternoon. The ambassador passed through the reception space and peeked into her own office, where she expected to see Daniel. There was a jacket hanging on the back of her chair and a box of donuts from Hole Universe on her display desk.

At least he got me something, Kelly thought, going in and opening the box. Other than crumbs, it was empty. Clearly she hadn't been expected, but then again, she hadn't sent any messages. She'd just assumed that Libby would have told the embassy staff that the vacation was over and the ambassador was returning to work.

"Where is everybody?" Kelly asked the ceiling.

"At the HEEL rally," Libby replied. "Donna was going to reserve the Meteor room at the Empire Convention Center, but Daniel and Walter were afraid they couldn't get a big enough crowd to make it look full. So they held the rally in the Little Apple to try to get a boost from the lunch trade. They'll be returning shortly."

"What's HEEL?" the ambassador asked.

"It's the Human Expatriates Election League," Libby explained. "Walter is their organizer on Union Station, and Daniel has gotten very involved. HEEL's message isn't entirely coherent, but Walter either wants to hold galaxy-wide elections for humans to establish their own government, or he's trying to move humanity to a hierarchically-based society. In either case, they want to throw off the yoke of Stryx domination."

"Why didn't you call me?" Kelly demanded, staring up at the ceiling. "Doesn't this qualify as your idea of an emergency? I could understand Daniel going in for something like this, but not Donna. And I saw her just a few days ago when she and Stanley brought us dinner."

"Everybody agreed not to disturb you while you were on vacation," Libby replied. "Besides, I'm sure that Daniel has his reasons which he'd rather explain to you himself than having me steal his thunder."

"At least tell me that they're not paying for it with the embassy budget," Kelly said, removing Daniel's jacket from her chair and hanging it on one of the guest chairs next to the desk.

"Not a single cred," Libby reassured her. "HEEL appears to be very well funded, and any additional expenses are being picked up by EarthCent Intelligence. Donna was going to offer free entry to her monthly mixer for people who attended the rally, but Blythe insisted on paying the tab to buy them tickets instead, so it won't cut into the embassy's petty cash fund."

"Wait a minute. EarthCent Intelligence is giving out free tickets to the EarthCent dance mixer to people who attend a political rally to replace EarthCent?"

"It shows a certain broadmindedness you don't see in many intelligence services. Of course, Blythe was one of my best students," Libby added proudly.

"I give up," Kelly said, sitting down at her display desk. "I wasn't really going to start working again until Monday, but since I'm here, I may as well start wading through my backlog of messages."

"Shouldn't you enjoy the weekend first?"

"Thanks to Libbyland, I'm all refreshed and ready for action. Besides, what could be worse than my junior consul and my best friend plotting to replace EarthCent. Go on. Give me the bad news first."

"There isn't any," Libby said, sounding slightly embarrassed.

"Really? That's great. Let's have the good news, then."

"Actually, there's just the one thing. EarthCent human resources agreed that the retroactive change to the paid maternity leave policy was improper, so your vacation time has been restored."

"All six months? Hah! That'll teach them to mess with me. Now if I get any pushback about being out on walkabout for a month, I can plaster it over with vacation time. What else?"

"Daniel and Donna did an excellent job covering for you with EarthCent, and of course, all of your friends and fellow diplomats knew you were on vacation so they didn't leave messages. By the way, the interview you recorded with Ambassador Srythlan went over very well. It didn't get the same ratings as the one with Dring, but I'm sure the Grenouthians were pleased with the results."

"Stop trying to change the subject," Kelly said, wagging her finger at nobody in particular. "Are you telling me that I was gone for a month and nobody even noticed?"

"They're back," Libby said, right before the outer door to the embassy office opened.

"Hello? Is somebody here?" Donna called. "I could have sworn I locked the door. We're going to have to sweep for bugs now."

"I'm in here," Kelly replied, getting up from the chair and going to meet her office manager. "It was locked when I arrived, which I thought was kind of funny, but I assumed there was a meeting going on or something."

"No, we were all at the rally. It was a huge success. The rest of them are headed over to the conference room at EarthCent Intelligence to edit the footage now. I imagine it will shoot Walter to the top of the HEEL ranks."

"Why does everybody want to help some guy who thinks the Stryx are oppressing us?" Kelly asked.

"To find out what's really going on," Donna replied.

Before Kelly could ask for an explanation, Donna pointed at her ear, indicating that there was an incoming call to the embassy. She moved to her desk, brought up the hologram Kelly recognized as the spreadsheet for her mixer, and entered something with a finger gesture.

"People are starting to call to confirm their reservations with the free tickets we handed out at the rally. I might have to get a bigger room for the next mixer," Donna said happily. "Oops, here's another one—I'm going be busy for a while. You should just run over to EarthCent Intelligence and see the recording."

"I'll do that," Kelly said, but Donna's attention had already shifted to another lonely-heart human. The ambassador gave her friend a goodbye wave just in case, and headed back out into the corridor. A few minutes later, she arrived at the offices of EarthCent Intelligence.

"They're in there," said a grouchy-looking young woman with a sword. "They didn't let me bring my rapier to the rally so I had to leave it here."

"I'm sure they didn't mean anything by it," Kelly replied automatically, walking up to the camera that covered the conference room door. All of the business with cameras and door buzzers seemed to her incredibly clunky compared to relying on Libby to identify visitors. But EarthCent Intelligence wasn't directly supported by the Stryx, and they used off-the-shelf hardware for many security functions.

"Welcome back," Clive said as Kelly entered the room. Everybody stopped what they were doing for a minute to voice their pleasure in seeing that the ambassador had returned from vacation. The ambassador's greeters included one young man whom she didn't recognize.

"Ambassador McAllister. Allow me to introduce Walter Dunkirk," Daniel said, bringing the two together.

"I've heard so much about you, Mrs. Ambassador," the HEEL organizer said.

"I'm afraid you have the advantage of me," Kelly replied. "I heard about you for the first time from Libby a few minutes ago, and she implied you were trying to put me out of a job."

"Not immediately," Walter protested.

"One month," Kelly continued, as if he hadn't spoken. "I go on vacation for one month, my junior consul joins a crackpot revolutionary movement, and nobody thinks it's worth disturbing me. Should I assume that HEEL was behind all of the political incidents that we discussed in my last—is this guy even trustworthy?"

"We're grooming Walter to be our first mole," Blythe told her. "He's going through the training camp now, and we're hoping that with this performance, he'll be called into HEEL headquarters to show the other organizers how it's done. They haven't had much success to this point from what we can tell."

"And you want to help them," Kelly said, crossing her arms and letting the sarcasm enter her voice. She was pretty steamed over finding herself so out of the picture.

"The HEEL organizers make some interesting points," Jeeves said. "And humans will have to take care of themselves eventually."

"And when did you join EarthCent Intelligence?" Kelly asked pointedly.

"He hasn't, but he's very keen on HEEL, and Clive doesn't have the heart to ask him to stop coming to the meetings," Blythe replied.

"It's great that you're here, Ambassador," Daniel said. "You'll be seeing the footage for the first time, while the rest of us know it from the live performance. We want to cut it down to about ten minutes, just the parts with the highest impact."

"And you're going to broadcast this?"

"No, ma'am," Walter said politely. "I'm going to submit it to HEEL headquarters as proof that I'm reaching the people and following the platform."

"Are there donuts in that box?" Kelly asked grudgingly, taking a seat at the table.

"I just picked them up," Shaina replied. "And I think the tea is ready by now.

Kelly tried to look nonchalant as she claimed a triple-chocolate donut, but her hand showed a visible tremor. She had wanted to set a good example for the children while they were on vacation, so other than the emergency supplies, she hadn't requested chocolate with any of their meal deliveries. It was inexplicable to her that none of her friends had read her mind and just brought some along. Not even Gwendolyn, and the Gem were chocoholics.

Shaina poured several mugs of freshly brewed herbal tea for the non-coffee drinkers and slid one over in front of Kelly. Daniel did something with the camera to interface it with the conference room display system, and an image of the central plaza area of the Little Apple popped up over the table. It wasn't a true hologram, since it was taken with one camera, but the display equipment used a series of holographic optical tricks to provide a frontal view from all angles.

"Thank you all for coming," Walter's hologram greeted the crowd. He was standing beneath a giant banner stenciled HUMAN EXPATRIATES ELECTION LEAGUE. A number of the people crowding in behind him in the image frame held signs with slogans, though the only one that caught Kelly's attention was brandished by Chance and read, "One human-derived sentient, one vote."

A hundred teenage girls began chanting, "HEEL, Walter, HEEL. HEEL, Walter, HEEL," which left Kelly with the impression he was either a rock star or a naughty puppy.

"Thank you. Thank you." Walter waved to individuals here and there in the crowd, making frequent eye contact with the camera and establishing a sort of intimacy with the viewers. The cheering and chants continued unabated.

"How did he become so popular with teenage girls?" Kelly asked.

"InstaSitter," Blythe replied. "Don't worry. It's not on the embassy budget."

Walter extended both of his arms and made some gentle patting motions with his hands, which the paid babysitter section of the crowd correctly interpreted as a request to quiet down.

"As you all know, I'm here today to talk about self-government for humans. It would be a violation of all I

210

believe in for me to simply present a political platform and tell you that this is the way it must be. Instead, I'm going to offer the principles of the Human Expatriates Election League for your approval, and I want you to let me know what you think."

The InstaSitters chanted a quick, "HEEL. Walter. HEEL."

"Thank you. Our first principle is that all sentients have a right to self-determination. Can I get a show of hands if you agree?"

Hundreds of hands went up, and the girls started chanting, "First Principle. Self-determination. First Principle. Self-determination."

Daniel hit pause. "Thoughts so far? Do we want to keep all of these chants in?"

"At least fast forward through them for now," Shaina said. "You could always make a director's cut later and put them back in."

"Kelly?" Daniel asked politely.

"Hrumph," the ambassador responded, her mouth full of chocolate donut.

Daniel restarted the playback.

"Thank you. Thank you," Walter repeated, making the same quieting gestures with his hands. "All of us here know how much our Stryx hosts have done for humanity. During my brief stay on Union Station, I've learned that many of you see this help as a growing debt, even though the Stryx may never present a bill. It's the debt of a child to a parent, but eventually, children grow up. When will humans grow up? Our second principle is that with self-determination comes responsibility. Humanity must take responsibility for itself. Do you agree?"

Enough hands surged upwards to make it obvious there was no need to poll for dissenters, but the response was less enthusiastic than for the previous question. The InstaSitters tried a chant of "Second Principle. Humanity must take responsibility for itself," but the length of the sentence got them out of sync with one another and they didn't try to repeat it.

"We understand that building a government takes time. But we also understand that beginnings are just as important as endings. A government without the consent of the governed is no place to start, and although I count EarthCent employees amongst my closest friends, they were picked for their jobs by the Stryx. Third principle. EarthCent is a building block for dependency, not self-government. A show of hands?"

Kelly was gratified to see that some more hands remained down, though the pre-paid teenagers and lonely-hearts voted as a block along with Walter. Whoever was operating the camera made a point of showing that support was spread throughout all age groups. The ambassador was momentarily surprised to see Peter Hadad and Ian Ainsley enthusiastically demonstrating their support, surrounded by like-thinking human vendors from the Shuk and the Little Apple. Then she remembered that the rally was an EarthCent Intelligence production.

"All of us can trace our recent roots back to Earth, including our artificial people. Some of us, myself included, grew up on Earth, but I'll wager that most of you have never voted in a human election. To be honest, you haven't missed much. The history of democracy on Earth is a story of wealth, celebrity, family name and incumbency. Fourth principle. Leadership should be open to anybody who can lead. Do you agree?"

Support for the forth principle was nearly unanimous, and since the InstaSitters couldn't decide what to chant, Daniel allowed the video to continue without pause.

"One person, one vote. What does that really mean?" Walter asked rhetorically. "On Earth, it meant that after the moneyed interests and the unelected elites picked their candidates, the people were allowed to choose best of the worst. Democracy? Yes. Self-government? Hardly. We say that government needs to be one person talking to one person. Not just a vote, but a permanent channel of communications. Fifth Principle. Answerability. Are you with me?'

The sea of hands went up again, and the girls began chanting, "Answerability. HEEL. Answerability. Walter." Daniel hit fast forward.

"Thank you. You all know that money talks and hot air dissipates. Our benevolent hosts have had tens of millions of years to develop a system to govern a large chunk of the galaxy. How do they keep the peace? With economic incentives, with the Stryx cred. You get what you pay for with government, and in the old Earth governments so well-documented by the Grenouthians, what you got was out of control borrowing and debts passed on to future generations. The fiscal and monetary sins of our governments were what forced the Stryx to step in and save us, costing us our independence. Sixth principle. A species in hock cannot stand."

Walter didn't even have to ask for a show of hands this time. Many of the Little Apple shoppers who had wandered over out of curiosity clapped without being paid, and the InstaSitters briefly chanted, "No Debt, HEEL. No Debt, Walter."

"So how do we build and finance a new form of government, an answerable form of government. A government that can't spend money it doesn't have and can't pay people more than their supporters believe they are worth. HEEL believes we have found that solution. Seventh Principle. Multi-level government. A government of relationships. Does that sound good?"

"Relationship Government," the girls chanted once or twice.

"What's he talking about?" Kelly subvoced to Jeeves, communicating over her implant so as not to interrupt the others.

"It's a pyramid scheme for government. Great potential for the person at the top," Jeeves replied in her ear.

"Thank you. Thank you," Walter said, requesting calm once again. That's when Kelly noticed that many of the older audience members were holding plastic cups with foam clinging to the sides, pretty clear evidence that free beer had played a major role in the turnout. "Now here's the key concept to the whole thing. The more of you who sign up today, the higher I'll rise in the government. The higher I rise, the closer YOU are to the top. Eighth Principle. Proximity equals power."

"Hold on," Kelly said, causing Daniel to pause the playback. "I get that a human pyramid can only have one person on top, I've been to the circus. But there's a limit to how many people can be in each layer before the ones at the bottom get crushed into donut fillings."

"Very well put," Clive said, poking his finger into a powdered jelly donut and bringing it out covered with raspberry jam. "Unfortunately, Walter has to work with what HEEL gives him. They're still developing their training materials. Just one iteration back, their idea was to bribe everybody into voting."

"What a bizarre hash of mismatched concepts," Kelly said. "If somebody actually tried electing a government like this, it would mean an instant dictatorship. Have we figured out who's behind HEEL yet?"

"That's what this is all about," Daniel said. "They've been recruiting their organizers through anonymous postings to job boards and using untraceable Thark accounts for transferring money. All Walter knows about his employers comes from the materials they deliver by a regular commercial service, no return addresses."

"Jeeves?" Kelly asked, hating herself for attempting the shortcut.

"Competitive information," the Stryx replied. "And the truth is, I'd just be making a high-probability guess. Somebody is doing a very good job covering their tracks."

Nineteen

A double section of the high ceiling in Mac's Bones re-tracted, leaving nothing but the atmosphere retention field between the pressurized hold and the vacuum of Union Station's open core. Aisha refused to look up as the alien craft came into view. Instead, she dropped to her knees and hugged Ailia with a ferocity that might have scared the child in any other situation. Beowulf patrolled around them in a tight circle, looking upset. Everybody was wearing their best clothes, but the mood was as somber as a funeral.

"It's a damned shame," Joe repeated to Paul for the tenth time since Gryph had alerted them to the approaching ship and its business a few hours earlier. "I know it's the best thing for the long run, but it's still a damned shame."

"Maybe it's better to get it over with now rather than five years down the road, but I doubt Aisha sees it that way," Paul replied, for perhaps the third time.

"You double-checked that this Baylit woman is telling the truth?" Joe asked Jeeves. The Stryx was ostensibly there as Paul's friend, but also to make sure that the volatile Vergallian wouldn't decide that the humans had offended her honor and try to start a shooting war in the hold.

"It's not even a secret at this point," Jeeves replied. "The Grenouthian news network has been broadcasting exclusive video of her forced landing on Farling Pharmaceutical's export orbital. The Vergallians never even acknowledged Farling traffic control, and I suspect she was disappointed when they capitulated without a fight. Of course, the Farlings have no vested interest in Vergallian wars of succession and would have gladly sold her the evidence for a suitable price."

The Vergallian captain's gig eased through the atmosphere retention field and began its descent. The vessel was only the size of Joe's tug, the Nova, but it was heavily armored and showed signs of repaired battle damage.

"If her transport for polite visits looks like that, I'd hate to see the mother ship angry," Woojin commented.

"I still can't believe she risked starting a war between the Empire of a Hundred Worlds and the Farlings based on a rumor," Kelly said. "I know the Vergallians take their honor seriously, but the Farlings are a much more advanced species. Besides, the military types must have a pragmatic side or they wouldn't have hired so many of you guys as mercenaries. Didn't one of you tell me you were in a Vergallian war that they halted when it went over budget?"

"Yes, but all of our experience was with the planetary forces on the tech-ban worlds," Clive replied. "Their fleet is a whole different culture. It rarely even visits the worlds on the tunnel network, and they don't use mercenaries. According to our friends in Drazen Intelligence, there's no love lost between the fleet and the larger royal houses. If it wasn't for the family relations and the economic ties, they'd probably be at war with each other."

"So this Baylit woman got evidence from the Farlings proving Ailia's family was defeated through cheating, and the royal house that engineered the war was outlawed and had to concede the kingdom?" Kelly speculated, recapping the snatches of conversation she'd overheard while she was also trying to help Aisha hold herself together. The whole thing had happened so suddenly that it was unbelievable, but perhaps as Paul had implied earlier, getting it over quickly was the best for everybody.

"The royal house that cheated had to concede their lives," Clive replied grimly. "Their own troops and mercenaries turned against them. The whole tech-ban system for preserving a feudal society on most of the Vergallian worlds falls apart if somebody sneaks advanced technology into a war. They all live in fear of undetectable drugs that can alter the course of a battle by degrading the performance of soldiers and their mounts, including those oversize birds they fly for air support. When you put war back on a medieval footing, there's nothing more important than the health of the army, mental and physical. Some of those Farling compounds can make a man see ghosts."

Kelly glanced around quickly to make sure the children weren't in earshot. "And Baylit survived when Ailia's family was massacred because she was off-world with the fleet?"

"She's not legitimate, you can tell by her name," Joe said. "You know the Vergallians live longer than humans, three hundred years or more if they don't get killed in a war or an accident. The men in the royal houses rarely marry before they're a hundred or so. Baylit is Ailia's half-sister through a consort her father had before marrying, but royal succession with the Vergallians is strictly through the distaff side."

"Sending an illegitimate son to the military was common practice in medieval times on Earth," Woojin contributed. "High ranking military have many of the same privileges as the royal houses on Vergallian worlds, though nobody ever forgets who is who."

"So this woman can rule in Ailia's name for now, but she can't seize power for herself?" Kelly asked in a low voice. Her reading about feudal times on Earth, both fiction and nonfiction, suggested that bad faith on the part of a guardian often led to regicide.

"That's right," Woojin reassured her. He had spent a large portion of his mercenary career on Vergallian worlds, and his familiarity with the royalty of the eastern nations on Earth helped him unravel the complex family structures of his alien employers. "It's rare for the Vergallian College of Heralds to grant guardianship of a royal heir to a relative who isn't related to the mother, but the circumstances are somewhat unique."

"They didn't want to offend a woman who commands the loyalty of a squadron of ships and has demonstrated that she isn't afraid to use it," Clive translated for Kelly. "We don't have great intelligence on the inner workings of the Vergallian empire, but it's not credible that a rogue house would have gambled on violating the tech-ban on their own initiative. It's more likely that both of the families involved were being used as pawns in a bigger game, but somebody made a fatal mistake by not taking Baylit into account."

The captain's gig settled onto the deck of Mac's Bones, where it looked badly out-of-place against the background of small traders and family-sized excursion craft. The front hatch popped open almost immediately, and four Vergallian marines emerged and formed a small honor guard for their captain.

Kelly gasped as Baylit stepped out of her craft, and then inhaled sharply again when the captain turned towards them. The ambassador's first look at the Vergallian's face showed a triangular mass of scar tissue extending from the jaw to the melted ear, leaving an artificial eye staring out of a reconstructed socket. But when she turned her good side to the waiting humans, Kelly saw a profile that looked like an artist's conception of Ailia projected some years into the future.

In accordance with Vergallian etiquette, Joe stepped forward and barred the captain's way.

"Permission to enter your territory," Baylit stated formally, though her tone and bearing left no room to imagine it was a request.

"Permission granted," Joe replied, unable to sound happy about it.

After completing the brief ritual, the Vergallian captain allowed her gaze to move away from Joe, and she quickly spotted Ailia peeking out from behind Aisha's back. Beowulf bristled as Baylit approached, but the woman showed no fear of the giant dog, and the corner of her mouth on the good side might even have twitched upwards. She stopped a pace away from the human woman, who was still kneeling with her back towards the unwelcome visitor, and allowed the Huravian hound to sniff her. Beowulf had been hoping it was all a mistake, but his nose told him the woman was Ailia's half-sibling for certain.

Aisha felt her Vergallian orphan go rigid in her arms and she realized the time had come. She rose slowly and faced Baylit, keeping her hands on Ailia's shoulders. The human woman's face was streaked with tears that she made no attempt to wipe away.

"Queen Ailia," the battle-scarred captain addressed the little girl formally. "I am Royal Protector Baylit, duly appointed by the College of Heralds."

"Royal Protector and elder paternal half-sister Baylit, I accept your authority," Ailia replied. It was a formulaic response that Banger had taught her after consultation with Libby. The transfer of power was completed in the two brief sentences, as was typical for Vergallian formalities.

"Did you know of my existence before today?" Baylit asked gruffly. She hadn't seen her father since shortly after Ailia was born, and she knew that the girl had been sent away for safe keeping when she was barely old enough to talk.

"Avidya, Andina, Adura, Baylit," Ailia half sang in response. "But I didn't know who any of the people were. It's just the end of a list of twenty-four names I was taught to recite at bedtime every night before my parents sent me here."

"Your mother included me in the last verse of your succession chant?" The burned face twisted with emotion, and Baylit crouched down to bring her eyes on level with the girl's. "Avidya was your mother, Andina and Adura were your two older sisters. You've already accepted me as the Royal Protector. Can you accept me now as your family?"

Ailia stepped forward and put her arms around the woman's neck, not hesitating to place her head on Baylit's damaged side and press her cheek against the old scar tissue. The Vergallian briefly stroked the little girl's hair, and then she straightened up again, keeping hold of one of Ailia's hands.

"As the Royal Protector and Ailia's sister, I thank you for taking care of her for us," Baylit said to Aisha.

Aisha blinked and bowed her head, but she couldn't think of anything to say.

"I can protect her better than you," Samuel declared in Vergallian, running up and seizing Ailia's free hand.

"I thank you also," Baylit said formally, but the boy wasn't interested in words.

"Stay with us," he begged the girl. "Banger will be so sad if you go that he'll probably turn himself off. And you know Beowulf only lets me ride on his back if you're there."

"Samuel," Kelly said, coming up and putting her hand on her son's head. "It's all been decided. It wouldn't be right for us to keep Ailia from her family now that they've found each other."

Samuel pulled on Ailia's hand as hard as he could, and though the girl looked at him sadly, she didn't let go of Baylit. For a moment, she was stretched between the Vergallian captain and Samuel. Then the boy's grip failed and he fell on the floor.

"Who needs a dumb girl anyway!" Samuel cried. Then he turned and fled off towards to the ice harvester, where he crawled underneath to hide. Banger dipped once in the direction of Ailia to say goodbye, and then the little Stryx followed the boy silently. Kelly turned to start after him as well, but Joe stopped her.

"Let him be for a bit," he said. "It's going to take time."

"You are the boy's parents?" Baylit asked. The McAllisters nodded their assent. The Vergallian woman reached in her boot and pulled out a small, sheathed throwing dagger, which she handed to Joe. "Please give this to the boy when he comes of age. The hilt bears my father's crest and it will grant him safe passage to Ailia's world if he chooses to visit."

"Thank you," Joe said, accepting the weapon and sliding it into his pocket before Kelly could object. "Your sister has been a good friend to our son. We're all going to miss her."

"And you are also the EarthCent Ambassador," Baylit stated, speaking directly to Kelly. "I thank you for taking my sister into your household. Please accept this as a token of my gratitude to EarthCent for dealing kindly with a friendless refugee." She reached into an inner pocket of her tunic and brought out a small black rectangle, which she pressed into Kelly's hand.

"Thank you," Kelly responded diplomatically, not having a clue whether the object was a hard candy or a miniature anti-personnel mine. "May I ask you something?"

"As long as I don't have to appear on your interview show," Baylit replied, a half-smile fleeing across her stern features. "I watched a recording of your interview with the Maker. We never knew such a war with AI took place."

"Did you find out that Ailia was on Union Station through her nurse?" Kelly asked. "It's been almost six months since she left Ailia in the studio, and I was wondering if she had a change of heart."

"The nurse remains on my to-do list," Baylit said coldly.

"Please, elder paternal half-sister," Ailia interrupted, intuitively understanding what her guardian meant. "If she hadn't abandoned me, I never would have come here and made friends with Samuel and all of the McAllisters."

"As my queen desires," Baylit replied grudgingly, glancing towards the ice harvester.

223

"Mist and I packed all of your stuff, Ailia," Dorothy said, dragging up a large duffle bag. "We added all of our souvenir holograms from Libbyland. Jeeves said he can get us copies."

Ailia tried to say something but ended up just swallowing. Kelly looked at the girl's white face and worried that she was going into shock. Baylit must have realized that the young queen's reserves were nearing an end, because she reached down and picked the girl up. A head nod brought one of her marines at a run. The soldier snatched up the duffle bag and took it back to the captain's gig.

"Permission to leave your territory," Baylit requested of Joe.

"Permission granted," Joe replied woodenly. Then he recovered his manners and snapped to attention, offering the Vergallian captain his sharpest salute.

Paul supported Aisha to keep her from collapsing as Baylit marched up the ramp of her gig. Ailia had one arm around her half-sister's neck as she looked back at the family who had taken her in, waving like mad with her free hand. Then the remaining marines entered the gig and the ramp closed after them. The ship began to rise a moment later, and the humans watched sadly as it cleared the atmosphere retention field, taking the little Vergallian girl away from them.

Twenty

"So you're saying that the Human Expatriates Election League is actually a front for Vergallian Intelligence?" a shocked Ambassador White asked Kelly. "But how could an advanced species be so incompetent at politics?"

"Consider it from the other side," President Beyer suggested. "They managed to recruit hundreds of innocent humans and artificial people to do their dirty work for them, and all it took was money. Even with the unworkable political platform, they still operated undetected for more than a month."

"I've been getting a crash course in Vergallian politics from our intelligence analysts, and I'm afraid we got lucky this time," Kelly said. "As with most of the aliens, the Vergallians hold a view of humanity which has been heavily influenced by Grenouthian documentaries. I've only watched a few of those myself, but I understand that they kind of make us out to be unsophisticated."

"That's putting it mildly," the President remarked. "The Grenouthians have a tendency to play up the darker episodes of human history for the sake of ratings. And they think we're idiots."

"But what made you decide to give the local HEEL organizer your backing?" Ambassador Oshi inquired. "When I saw the video of your assistant consul introducing that man at the anti-EarthCent rally on Union Station, I had to wonder if you'd snuck off on a long vacation."

"That was an undercover operation," Kelly replied hastily, hoping the half-truth would limit her blush response. "My assistant consul was working with EarthCent Intelligence to bolster the standing of the local HEEL organizer. They planned to infiltrate him into the leadership of the movement to find out what was going on."

"And how did you discover it was the Vergallians?" Ambassador Fu asked.

"As I said, we got lucky," Kelly replied. Then she offered the explanation she'd concocted with Blythe and Clive. "I can't share all of the operational details, but our intelligence people did obtain holo-cube residue from a HEEL communication and had it analyzed by Drazen Intelligence."

"Ah, I'll have to remember that," Ambassador White said. "I never realized holo-cubes leave a residue."

"And it's not like we were expecting this attempt," President Beyer added. "I want to know what our intelligence people make of the motive?"

"It's complicated," Kelly replied. "Part of it has to do with Vergallian royal factions and a split between the imperial family and the deep space fleet that we're just beginning to understand. The Vergallian ambassadors we know from the Stryx stations are all members of the imperial faction, but the smaller royal houses and the off-network colonies and worlds are solidly behind the fleet. When you consider that there are hundreds of populated worlds involved, there's plenty of room for plots and counter-plots."

"Hundreds?" Belinda asked. "I thought it was exactly a hundred worlds."

226

"There are two hundred and seventy-one Vergallian domains recognized by their College of Heraldry, and another eighty-nine, if you include the dwarf planets and terraforming projects," Kelly replied instantly. If there was one good thing about having vivid nightmares, it was that she always remembered the facts that popped up. Where they came from initially, she hadn't a clue.

"That translates into a lot of Vergallians," Ambassador Fu remarked. "You'd think they'd have enough to do looking after their own affairs."

"Blythe promises me that you'll all be receiving a detailed report as soon as the analysts finish cross-checking their conclusions with Drazen Intelligence," Kelly said. "Their preliminary recommendation is that we remove the temptation for other species to meddle in our politics."

"Meaning that nature abhors a vacuum," President Beyer observed. "But we have no mandate to extend EarthCent beyond our current role as a diplomatic service, and attempting to do so might actually make us guilty of the imaginary crimes the HEEL organizers were attributing to us."

"We could offer to help human colonies establish local elections," Ambassador Oshi suggested.

"That brings me to the second reason I called this meeting," Kelly said. "I believe you all received a report from EarthCent Intelligence earlier today which details the development of independent human communities on the open worlds of the Dollnicks, Drazens and Verlocks."

"It's five in the morning here," Ambassador Tamil replied. "I was already asleep when it came in and I'm barely awake now. In other words, I haven't read it yet."

"I'm sorry, Raj," Kelly said. "I swear I'll schedule the next meeting at a better time for you."

"I believe I can summarize the report for you, Ambassador Tamil," Belinda offered. "The humans on open worlds are going native. They've not only adopted the technology of their hosts, but also their management structures, attitudes, and even a facsimile of their diets."

"Don't blame the Dollnicks for spoon worms," Ambassador Fu said. "Those are a Korean delicacy."

"I think the greater point here is that we're in no position to suggest to our fellow humans what form of government best suits their situation," President Beyer stated. "I view the willingness of the human leaders to meet with their counterparts from other independent communities positively, and I fully approve of EarthCent Intelligence picking up the tab for hosting such an event."

"Do we need to vote on it?" Belinda asked.

"Not unless you want to," the President replied.

"Ever since I got back from, uh, lunch," Kelly stuttered, barely catching herself in time from spilling the beans about her vacation, "I've been thinking about reassigning my assistant consul to meeting with humans rather than aliens. If humanity is going to continue developing in different directions, then maintaining good relations amongst ourselves should fit under the umbrella of a diplomatic service. We'd become the fools the Vergallians think we are if we spend all of our time talking with the neighbors as our own household descends into chaos."

"What a nice way of putting it," Ambassador Zerakova said. "There's an old Russian proverb that expresses much the same sentiment."

"Yes, I especially liked the part about getting back from lunch," President Beyer added dryly, causing Kelly to cringe. The man seemed to have developed a second sight since taking over as president. "But before we rush to invite any self-governing human communities to take a seat at the EarthCent table, I want to remind you all that the Stryx will not be picking their leaders."

"Isn't that a good thing if we want to move towards genuine self-sufficiency?" asked Ambassador White.

"Yes and no," President Beyer replied. "Do any of you know why the Stryx picked you for the diplomatic service, and what qualified you to become an ambassador?"

"I'm good with numbers."

"I'm very organized."

"I do well on standardized tests."

"Yes, I'm sure those are all very useful skills, but as it happens, I hired a Thark consulting firm to analyze how the Stryx have been making their choices," President Beyer continued. "I thought it might come in handy for a future president."

"You turned over our personnel files to the Tharks?" Kelly asked.

"No, they were able to base their analysis on public information, since all of us are rather high profile individuals in the human context. I could draw this out and bury you in data like the Tharks buried me, but in the end, it came down to two factors for all of us."

"And it wasn't standardized tests?" Svetlana guessed.

"First, we aren't megalomaniacs. In fact, according to the Tharks, we're about as opposite as you can get from being power hungry without straying into terminal indecisiveness. Second, we're empathetic with aliens and AI. It's much easier to find humans who empathize with puppies than with aliens, and even the advanced species have difficulty relating to AI as fellow sentients."

"I do care about aliens and AI, and puppies too," Belinda said. "I can see why it's important for ambassadors, though I'd like to believe we all brought more than that to the table. But why should it be important for the leaders of self-governing human communities?"

"That's exactly the point," the president replied patiently. "When the Stryx appointed me to this job, every one of you privately told me you were relieved it wasn't you. If we start making the leaders of these new communities equal partners in EarthCent, they're going to want to be considered for the highest posts. At the same time, they'll likely see themselves as representatives of their constituents rather than of humanity as a whole. Unlike Belinda and the rest of us present, they may not be able to empathize with all of the aliens and AI, or even with puppies. We aren't at the point where we can afford to have tone-deaf humans representing Earth to the rest of the galaxy."

"There's something in that," Svetlana said. "If humans are really going native on these planets then they'll likely end up with some of the same biases as the aliens who they're emulating, but without the empires to back it up. I'll need some time to think about this."

"I don't see the harm in all of us focusing some resources on outreach to human communities on open worlds, but I agree the next step will require careful thought," Carlos added. "Maybe a parallel system would be best."

"Then let's leave it there and we'll talk next month," Kelly suggested. "I have a graduation ceremony to attend."

The ambassadors all signed off of the holo-conference, and in some cases, crawled back into bed. Kelly immediately headed home for Mac's Bones where the latest class of EarthCent Intelligence agents was graduating.

After the ceremony and picnic, the leaders of EarthCent Intelligence remained behind to hear Kelly's feedback from the steering committee and to polish off the leftovers. Dorothy took charge of Blythe's twins, and the three of them did their best to cheer up Samuel, who was still moping around a week after Ailia's departure.

"I swept the area again after the recruits and their guests left," Clive mentioned offhandedly. "Can't be too careful these days."

"I'd forgotten that the Vergallians tried to sneak an undercover agent into your first training camp," Kelly admitted. "I wonder what would have happened if Beowulf hadn't spotted him."

"I wonder what would have happened if Baylit hadn't given you that data cache," Lynx said. "Did you tell the steering committee about her?"

"No. I felt a little bad hiding it from them, and Baylit didn't say anything about keeping it confidential, but why take chances? The Stryx know obviously, since Jeeves is the one who decoded it for us, but otherwise, it's just the people at this table."

"We scrubbed most of the details before passing the data on to our analysts, so even if the Vergallians get a copy of the report, it should leave them guessing as to where our information came from," Clive informed her. "Baylit clearly suspects that Vergallian Intelligence played a role in the war that caused her father's death, and there's no love lost between their navy and their spies in any case."

"At least you were able to take Ailia on a nice vacation before she had to leave," Blythe added. "Paul told me she went off with plenty of holo-souvenirs to remember everyone by. He also said he's going to start working with

Jeeves to design some new tourist attractions for those abandoned decks."

"Sometimes I think that the Stryx get bored just like the rest of us," Kelly commented. "Libby said they have some bugs to work out before she opens to the general public, but she's hoping to make her theme park into a high-volume tourist attraction."

"You kept insisting Libby had some underhanded motive for the whole thing whenever we visited you," Blythe followed up in a teasing voice. "Have you figured it out yet?"

"Well, I haven't quite fit the wastewater treatment deck into my theory, but I'm pretty sure the idea was to teach us to avoid the traps that the former residents of the abandoned decks fell into," Kelly replied. "Dring mentioned that the species which lived in the exoskeleton suits, the Plangers, skipped directly from their stone age to high tech because some well-meaning aliens handed them technology on a silver platter. I wonder if the Stryx worry that we've been pulled forward too far too fast."

"Maybe she started us off with the sewer deck to show that you can't always improve on nature," Joe suggested.

"I'll bet that's it." Kelly took a sip from her beer and expanded on her thesis. "What other point could there be to meeting Marvin the ghost other than to show us that eternity is no prize. Instead of becoming gods, they left their bodies behind to become wards of the Stryx. Now poor Marvin is happy to get a job as a tour guide to help the years go by and contribute something to their overdue rent."

"Beautiful sculpture gardens," Blythe commented. "Did you remember to ask Libby about that foldable table, Joe?"

"Never mind that now," Kelly pressed onwards. "The message of the deck with the exoskeletons was obvious. I always wondered why the advanced species don't have robots do more for them, but it's mainly AI who build a lot of mechanicals. Those Plangers became so obsessed with making everything safe and easy that they ended up with lives not worth living."

"And the pretend business?" Blythe asked. "I can't get over the fact that the whole species went in for it."

"I asked Libby about them after we got back, and that one has a happy ending," Kelly said. "Rather than dying off, they did one of those back-to-nature things, like the Kasilians. Libby said they're mainly farmers and small craftsmen now, and they have strict laws against automation."

"I don't think any of the humans we met on our honeymoon are heading towards those problems," Woojin said. "They didn't hesitate to tell us that they thought the Dollnicks, Drazens or Verlocks were the examples we should all be following."

"So if educational entertainment is edutainment, what's an educational vacation?" Lynx asked.

"Edu-cation?" Kelly ventured, putting the syllables together. "No, that doesn't work. They blend too well."

"So what did you all think of my graduating class?" Thomas asked. "I did a survey while they were eating, and all of them are willing to come back for advanced training. Chance and I have lots of ideas for new field exercises, and I bet Herl would loan us some Drazen trainers if we asked."

"What sort of ideas?" Blythe asked suspiciously. There had been some complaints from local merchants about the creative missions the artificial people assigned, including an incident in which a pair of recruits successfully drained the deep fryer at the Burger Bar during the height of the dinner rush. They might have escaped undetected if they hadn't tried sneaking out with the hot oil in a mop bucket, thoroughly cooking the mop.

"Advanced espionage techniques, like deception, hacking and misinformation," Thomas replied, in the same tone he might have read a menu. "I've been studying the library archives on the history of espionage and I think that our focus on recruiting sources is far too conservative. It's probably because we've been concentrating on business intelligence that we can sell, but I've been talking with Jeeves..."

"Jeeves?" Kelly interrupted, her voice rising. "Aren't the Stryx supposed to be neutral in all of this?"

"Neutral buoyancy," Jeeves declared, after floating silently up to the table and causing Kelly to jump. "It's the whole trick to sneaking up on people." He set down a plastic box full of glasses and pulled one out to display the Libbyland logo to everybody. "Special delivery from the gift shop, compliments of the management."

"My other theory is that Libby made up the whole theme park to try to keep you out of trouble," Kelly addressed the Stryx.

"There's something to that as well," Jeeves admitted. "I just can't get excited about running around the multiverse like the other young Stryx. What's so interesting about an infinite number of barely differentiated realities? You could get lost and not even know it. Oops, everybody forget I said that."

"Forgotten," Thomas declared. He'd taken his hero literally and wiped the comment from his memory. "So, am I authorized to start running an advanced course for the training camp?"

"I don't see why not," Clive replied. "But we're going to need to hustle to replace the agents we're losing."

"What do you mean?" Kelly demanded. "Losing how?"

"You tell her," Clive said to his wife. "It's your family."

"Well, I've been trying to talk her out of it, but it looks like Chastity is sort of going into competition with us," Blythe said. "I should have known something was up when she left Tinka in charge of day-to-day operations at InstaSitter after she got back from her honeymoon on Earth, but we were all just happy to see her taking it easy for a change. It turns out she was preparing to launch a new business."

"She's going to start a private spy service?" Lynx asked.

"Sort of," Blythe said. "Apparently, there's so much re-cycled fiber on Earth that people can print the news on paper every day. Chastity fell in love with the whole thing and she's been working in secret to launch the first human galactic news service."

"Chastity is going to print newspapers in space?" Kelly asked in astonishment.

"She wanted to, but the economics just don't work," Blythe replied. "Her idea is to gather and report the news that humans care about and to use the Stryxnet to deliver subscriptions to tabs or anything else that can display text and pictures. She's already made a deal with the Stryx, and we just found out that she's poaching some of our best intelligence analysts for her start-up staff."

"The Union Station Times?" Joe guessed.

"The Galactic Free Press."

"How is it a business if it's free?" Thomas asked.

"It's not free," Blythe said. "That's just the name."

"So it's disinformation," the artificial person concluded. "But why does she want to deceive humans?"

"It's an expression from human history," Kelly explained. "A free press, one that isn't controlled by the government, is supposed to protect the citizens from their elected officials doing whatever they want and lying about it."

"But we don't have a government," Thomas protested.

"We will someday," Kelly replied. "Human history might have played out differently if we had invented the free press before the government, so maybe Chastity is on the right track. I think it's a great idea. I'm tired of getting my news from the Grenouthian network."

Sprawled beneath the table, his limbs twitching and his eyes darting about below closed lids, Beowulf was experiencing a race memory from the Earth-born half of his previous incarnation. He saw a boy on a bicycle pull a large bone from a sack on his back and throw it towards the porch of a house. Beowulf felt himself leap high in the air and catch it in his mouth, but instead of the pleasant smooth texture and taste of a bone, it grew soggy and inky as he chewed on it. Somebody came out of the house yelling, and the Huravian hound woke up with a bad taste in his mouth, wondering if he had eaten too much at the graduation party.

No, that couldn't be. In fact, now that he thought of it, he was hungry again.

EarthCent Ambassador Series:

Date Night on Union Station

Alien Night on Union Station

High Priest on Union Station

Spy Night on Union Station

Carnival on Union Station

Wanderers on Union Station

Vacation on Union Station

Guest Night on Union Station

Word Night on Union Station

Party Night on Union Station

Review Night on Union Station

Family Night on Union Station

Book Night on Union Station

LARP Night on Union Station

About the Author

E. M. Foner lives in Northampton, MA with an imaginary German Shepherd who's been trained to bite bankers. The author welcomes reader comments at e_foner@yahoo.com.

You can sign up for new book announcements on the author's website - IfItBreaks.com

Lightning Source UK Ltd.
Milton Keynes UK
UKHW041352310320
361126UK00002B/760